THE *GINOSKO* ANTHOLOGY 2

edited by Robert Paul Cesaretti

MadHat Press
Asheville, North Carolina

MadHat Press
MadHat Incorporated
PO Box 8364, Asheville, NC 28814

The material in this anthology is selected from the ezine
GinoskoLiteraryJournal.com
by Editor Robert Paul Cesaretti

ISBN 978-0-9885490-6-7 (paperback)

Cover art: "Full of Grace" by Delisa Sage
Book and cover design by MadHat Press

www.GinoskoLiteraryJournal.com
www.MadHat-Press.com

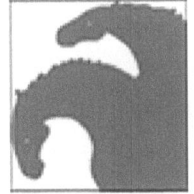 

ginosko

A word meaning
to perceive, understand, realize, come to know;
knowledge that has an inception,
a progress, an attainment.
The recognition of truth from experience.

CONTENTS

FERAL
~ Michael Cadnum

Most of the year, the riverbed is empty.
Feral dogs race along the gentle slope,
and this is where we abandon refrigerators,
obsolete computers, and half-burned mattresses,
and, if we have nothing, this is where we live.

The mop drying on the side porch, the blouse
hanging on a clothesline: things like
the way they are.
A pony in the cul-de-sac,
trudging around in a circle:
you can rent a ride and clop along
the sawdust strewn around the street-end.
It's a journey like many others, a word written

on glass. You parked under my window,
your new four-door a box of a solitude.
The speck of your cigarette
was all you were. Not simply all
that could be seen. This was
you, feeding yourself the dark.

SHE IS CAPTURED
~ Susan Niz

The sun sets behind her
She stands there like a windmill,
arms outstretched
No cares of the world hang in her profile
or her illuminated murmurs
of russet hair

A hedge of sumac blazes coolly to her side
a smattering of tinted wicks

Her long dress brushes the browning grass,
toes hidden in their coolness

She has dirt on her hands,
dust of crumbled yellow oak in her hair,
and the fallen torch of a maple between her fingers

She is captured

She blocks the setting sun
She quenches all memory
of sorrow with her bold, accidental nature

As if she could change the whole world,
there in the yard
amongst the discarded papery leaves

Her gaze collides with the fresh inferno of fall
reflecting only wonder and happenstance
with a glow

As if she could change the whole world,

She just did

fleshbone, what might have been
~ Sarah Dawson

Autumn
leaves of treachery
have fallen on soft, wet earth.
Trampled into an umber pulp of fleshy dirt in salty rains.

Under,

a bog,
a lonely skeleton stripped of veins
remains,
just sharp bones broken.

in the dark,
wait for reason.

There is so much winter before the next change of season.

FLIGHT
~ Jeanne Blum

We wander along the dune crest, following meandering sand lines, wave markers; little holes, once bubbles speckle the dune's lake side. With our bared feet the same size, we leave almost matching footprints, dry-colored ones on the dark sand, wet-colored ones on the dry. Farther inland the dunes rise up, a gentle clutter of congregating grass. Our loose sweatshirts and jeans, rolled up to mid-calf, flap wildly. The autumn breeze combs our hair, caresses our faces, fills our nostrils with the scent of clean sand, fresh, clear water, pushes the massed grey-tinged clouds in streams across the reflected sky. The great green-blue lake lashes roaring three-foot waves. We dodge them, easily laughing, as they lap gently at our ankles. Stripe-necked sandpipers scatter on chopstick legs, leaving mazes. Herring gulls swirl above, glide through invisible dance patterns, dip abruptly to light amidst the foamy waves. We open our flapping sails to the breeze to take it all in, to pour ourselves all out, to become grains of sand underfoot, crystal jewels of sparkling foam, almost imperceptible whirs of gulls' wings.

At Heart, Speed . . .
~ E. M. Schorb

At heart, speed is about being where you are going sooner than you can get there, and putting it all behind you. As you hurry forward to get where you are going, much is dropping behind, falling away from your frontal interest, as it were. If you were as fast as an atom, say, you could probably spin back and pick up some of what you have left behind and so take it with you as you propel forward, wherever that is now—for we have thoroughly muddled the issue in having gone back to pick up what was left behind because in having gone back we have made back forward, forward back. At heart, speed is an attempt to avoid as much as possible until we get to something we may or may not have in mind and stop there, but of course as we arrive there we find that we have just left and are now on our way to something that resembles in its lack of interest to us all that we have attempted to leave behind, so, in a sense, we are going backward, or, we should be going backward, toward what we wanted to get to in the first place. At heart, speed is our heart beating and speeding its beat until it has run out of beats. At heart, then, speed is our heart excitedly beating a trail to its end.

THE INTEMPERATE
~ Adam Burnett

Madame Desiree sighed heavily and thought about her last day on earth. She stared absently at the cool reflection in the water before her; she watched as the usually leveled line of her tiny mouth melted somewhat into a slight frown. Her skin was so smooth and white it was almost indistinguishable from the unlimited sky painted overhead. She hadn't always been this young, though; in fact, she could remember a time when she had been quite old, with skin like crumpled parchment. She thought of the line she had spoken from the last role she had ever played, and it came to her with such vividness that for a moment she actually believed she could feel the hot lights baking her skin, hanging above her like man-made stars.

> *"When the curtain goes down, I want to know that the role has ended, I want myself to return to me as though it had just been off to the side a little, waiting in the wings and re-evaluating. I want to join with that self and become whole".*

Another sigh escaped her lips and this time it swept her away.

< >

From the view from her bed all she could see was the massive oak dresser that seemed to stretch away from her the way she imagined the dining table would have at the Last Supper, had one stood and looked from one end to the other. On it were several little trinkets, a necklace, an eggshell hairbrush to which clung a few random hairs, wiry strands the colour of desert rocks bleached after eons in the sun, and a bottle of perfume so old it had lost its original smell completely, fading into a kind of generic non-smell. She knew this, of course (smell is one of the senses it seems that never quite loses its sharpness no matter how old one gets, unlike sight and hearing, which she reckoned

21

had begun fading decades ago). She kept it now only as a physical memory, for it recalled to her the days of her youth. Years ago the sight of that brush would have caused a wash of worry to course over her; the thought of losing hair like that, back then, was unthinkable. Now that it had actually happened, she realized the pointlessness of any concern in the first place. In fact, it might have been the worrying itself that had caused the hair to fall out. Her head shook silently as she considered this small irony, but not because she felt moved to do so; the old woman shook her head at everything these days, in fact it seemed that it never stopped shaking. It was forever wavering back and forth, as though unceasingly asserting just how much she disagreed with the situation. The truth was, she was just old. Or was it?

< >

She glanced up at the single unadorned light bulb that hung directly overhead, and she immediately wished she hadn't. Light bulbs always reminded her of the word *bulbous* and that always made her think about the pill. A gush of saliva immediately secreted into her mouth and she cringed slightly. In reflex her right hand arose to meet a clump of her remaining hair, and she twisted it gently around her forefinger; now that it had entered her mind it would be damn near impossible to let it out again. And really, why shouldn't it? After all, she did need it. Certainly not to the degree that she needed water, or oxygen, but it really wasn't too far off, was it? No, she assured herself, it wasn't just a simple want; it was a definite need, and that, in a nutshell, was the whole problem.

< >

The pill was in her head now; it was embedded into her brain like a long-ago-hammered nail; it had been there so long it was rusted with time and age; to try to remove it now would be worse that simply leaving it there. But this time she was determined. Bulbous.

Her mind pushed around the corner of her room and down the hall like an epic film's final revealing camera dolly, slow and forceful, forever controlled. She watched in her mind's eye as she came to the door at the end of the hall, stretched out a set of withered grape-vine fingers and pushed the door ajar. And then she was in, inside the pristine purity of the bathroom, surrounded by all things white and porcelain. Madame Desiree, that is, the real Madame Desiree, the one still in her bed, glanced up at the glass of water and fizz resting at the end of that long hard wooden dresser. *Teeth. Yes, that was it,* she thought, the bathroom always reminded her of teeth, equally white and just as easily cleanable and chippable.

Immediately she was back in the bathroom. Her hands were reaching up to the medicine cabinet, trying to find the latch that would lead her to relief. The lightbulb hanging above. Bulbous. Her hand kept reaching, kept moving but so slowly, as if encased in glass. She watched as those weak and feeble fingers tried to pry open the cabinet, having been unable to master the latch. They pawed at the cabinet, slapped it, began beating it with clenched fists, and she was screaming and crying, or trying to but all that came out was a pathetic whimper. Suddenly, and without warning, the hand turned and slapped herself in the face.

Back in bed, she felt that slap. It was not the first time she had come out of such a trance by such a method. Sometimes it was the only way. Even when she was younger, when her mind had been much more acute than it was now, she had occasionally required a taut slap cross the face in order to draw her out of one of her roles. It was too easy for her to lose herself completely.

Back in bed she felt the heat across her face. She swore she could feel each splayed digit and the crimson mark it had painted there, but at the same time she knew that this was probably her imagination. But one thing was not make-believe. The craving was still there. Her little day-dream had done nothing to dispel that desire.

The craving she felt now was nothing new; she had known it for years, decades even, but in the last remaining years it had grown sharper and sharper. She found herself constantly taunted by that pink button of a pill; it shouted out to her, called to her by the very knowledge of its existence. Her mind and body ached for its liberation, and these desires tunnelled into her head as an imploded geyser into the earth, digging, rearranging, negating all other designs.

And what could she do, really? What could one in her situation do? Was there anything to do when one was truly locked in a vacancy?

She sat there for a long time, sometimes closing her eyes and sometimes just staring off into nothingness. For how long she sat she had no idea; she kept no clocks in the house and hadn't for years. It was her contention that her wrinkled skin and careful step were reminder enough that her time on this earth was bounded by a limit; she certainly didn't need something whispering *tick...tock...tick...tock* over her shoulder twenty four hours a day. She guessed it couldn't have been that long, though, because she had yet to feel the inevitable pangs of hunger that she knew to usually strike her around the hour of noon. But she did want a drink, and badly.

For a brief moment she considered simply downing the glass of water that rested just a few feet away on the end of the dresser, but the sight of her own gummy teeth resting in the bottom of the glass was enough to dispel that thought quickly enough. Even still...

Damn did she hate to have to walk down to the bathroom. She absolutely *musn't* taste of that pill today, not today! *But could she really abstain? Was it even possible?*

She certainly couldn't remember all lines of dialogue she had been required to say (indeed it was questionable as to whether or not she could even remember the roles themselves), but occasionally one or two would pop into her head. It was from a play she had done, centuries ago, in which she had told the crowd *"The proximity of a desirable thing tempts one to overindulgence. On that path lies danger."* And she had always had her pills right by her side, hadn't she. Just waiting for her to reach out and pluck one up, like Eve in that primal garden. She tried to recall the name of the play from which the line had come but found she absolutely couldn't. It would be right on the tip of her tongue, balanced there sitting and waiting only for her to put some air behind it, and then it would be gone. Kind of like the way she was imagining taking that pill. It would be there, stuck to her tongue by equal amounts of saliva and desire, and then it would be gone.

This time that *push* down the hall was for real, her joints creaking like flaking iron fences and her greyed hair flowing out behind her like ripped threads of a ghostly costume, a spirit returning from stage left for the final closing act.

< >

Staring in the bathroom mirror only made her think of the pill all the more, and it wasn't because she knew it to be sitting on the other side, just a tiny piece of glass separating her and that other self, but because looking into her own eyes confirmed how *tired* she was. Her eyes were big and round and seemed to be the only thing on her body that had any real *life* left. But even yet they were bloodshot, misted red; one might even go so far as to say *pink*. She stared at that reflection and tried her best to concentrate on it as she ran the tap for a moment, letting the water cool, and then slowly filled the glass to the brim. She took a long cool, satisfying sip, her gaze never leaving her own eyes the entire time. *Her eyes, so...bulbous.*

Staring so intently into that mirror, things began to change. Her longing seemed to twist the very air between her and that tiny thing, manipulating the very atoms of empty space the way heat over a fire will ripple all above it. It was as though she was actually seeing through the glass mirror of the cabinet, or was she just seeing through herself? Into the cabinet and into herself. And the two fed off of each other, she knew, working together to create a pathetic and pitiable symbiosis. One could not, it seemed, have survived so long without the other. The pills would have gone to waste and she would have gone to the nuthouse, certainly, but here they both were, old friends who had together seen many *other* friends long lowered into the earth. *The box.* She thought of *that* box, the wooden kind that is, and then about

25

the one before her. She knew within this one lay many things, but there was always one that stood out. A narcotic gum-drop the colour of cotton candy, amidst tubes and dusted jars of pre-storm sky hue, potions and lotions collected over a lifetime, trophies footnoting to conquered ailments. In the other box, who knew? *Not much,* she was almost certain, *not much.* But only *almost* certain, not one hundred percent. She continued to stare at the mirror. *Bulbous.*

Uncertainty.

Finally she pried her hands away from the cold porcelain of the bleached white sink. They were painfully cold; again she had no idea how long she had been standing there, but judging by the way the joints of her hands flared up she guessed it to be quite a while. After much deliberation, and many attempts to actually do so, she finally managed to draw her gaze away from the mirror. She glanced left, at the crimson shower curtains that hung off to the side, separating one part of her routine from another, that of the toilet, which to her represented purging, and the shower, which was a tool for cleansing. She thought about the shower curtain and the way it bunched itself against the bathroom wall all the way back to her bedroom. Once there she settled in, leaned her head against the back pillow, folded her hands across her chest and felt herself slowly drifting off to sleep.

Her last breath pushed out from her stomach like the sigh from an aged pair of bellows, collapsed and forgotten, an original sound that seemed to contain all words the woman had ever spoken, a resonance comprised of all manners of desire and need. A final noise that remained a plea forever unanswered. Evening had come, and around her the lights of her house dimmed, lowered to nothingness by some unseen hand. Her younger self bowed to a wash of imagined applause.

STING
~ Alix Reeves

Frank leaned back in his studio chair and exhaled from his cigarette. He liked watching as the smoke curled and lifted toward the dark ceiling. He followed its slow-motion undulation as it joined and collected with cigarette smoke from his previous cigarettes to form an indoor horizon. Years of hosting radio had honed his timing; he knew without having to glance that there were forty-five seconds remaining in his break, prompting the red light on the panel to flash chaotically, indicating that he was, indeed, back on air.

The excitement of being on the radio had never left him. Most radio veterans bemoaned the lack of the old thrill, the thrill of knowing that one's voice would carry over most of a given county, that any mistake or lack of judgment would be heard almost instantaneously by hundreds of thousands of listeners. Frank considered himself fortunate for his still very real fear of blowing it on the air. His fear of using the wrong word or sounding less-than-knowing or of allowing a profane word to slip out into the land of sound.

Radio had found Frank; it was not a field he'd set out to conquer. His show was conceived by an offhand remark he'd made to Jim the program director, never intending it as a pitch. Having screened calls for years, he was happy with the meager salary and dependable hours.

Frank and Jim had been half-listening to a political call in show in Jim's office when a caller began a most entertaining, albeit insane rant.

While he listened to the guy, Frank spoke out compulsively, "Why do we always cut off the crazy callers? Listen to that guy go, Jim. Now, *that* makes for good radio."

"You could have something there. Crazy fuckers do keep things interesting." Jim said as he smirked and sat back in his chair.

Two weeks later Jim approached him with what would become one of the most syndicated radio talk shows ever, *The Frank Sound Show.*

When Jim made the suggestion, Frank had dismissed him immediately, assuming he was up to a prank when he'd offered him the slot. "Have my own show? You fucking with me?"

"Nope. The nine to one a.m. slot is yours. Thing is, you've got to follow the format."

"I'm afraid to ask; what *is* the format?"

"It's your idea, actually: keep the crazies on the air, egg them on, Frank, support any weird notion they bring up, be the one guy in the universe who not only listens to them, but offers them back-up. Make up shit. In two weeks of air time you'll be a pro."

His first night on felt like a disaster. Frank's ratings indicated otherwise; he wasn't a huge success, but for the late-night-early-morning slot, his numbers were notable. Over time, the numbers grew and suddenly his show was being offered more syndication deals than any other in radio history.

The most unexpected part was that his callers did all the work; he simply substantiated whatever the hell they said, hoping that by doing so they would unveil their darkest secrets, their most off-kilter beliefs or unheard-of propensities. And the formula worked.

"Hey Frank, this is Cliff from Riverside, I sent you an email attachment last week, did you get it?"

Thursday nights proved to be the most rewarding, callers like Cliff seemed to come out of the woodwork. Frank didn't know what it was about Thursdays in particular, what caused these lonely people to be more drawn than ever to his show, but he knew to be ready.

"Refresh my memory Cliff. Honestly, I get a boatload of email attachments."

"Oh yeah Frank sure, it was a picture that my buddy from D.C. sent me. He was let go from his Smithsonian job and I suppose he was pissed and just took it with him when he left, or a copy of it, I'm not sure…"

Frank interrupted, sensing the caller's drifting dialogue, "What was the photograph of, Cliff?"

"Dr. Mengele and Sir Winston *fucking* Churchill..." A loud beep interrupted Cliff's profanity. Frank could see Kyle, his screener, laughing his head off in the dim light of his booth.

Frank chuckled. "Hey Cliff, you're gonna have to keep it clean."

"Sorry, Frank, I get carried away, anyway it's a picture of Dr. Mengele and Winston Churchill...chatting in a Paris café. Keep in mind, Frank, this picture precedes Photoshop..."

"*My.... my.... my.*" Frank allowed a few beats for effect. "Cliff, are you suggesting you have evidence to show that these two men actually met? That Dr. Mengele, a Nazi physician who willingly conducted torturous experiments on Jewish victims, met with Sir Winston Churchill? In Paris?"

"Oh yeah, and *during the occupation*, Frank. Oh, and it gets worse; if you look real close at the picture, you can see that they're *holding hands under the table.*"

Frank embraced the silence, allowing it to add importance to Cliff's story. Letting out an audible and long breath, Frank continued in a grave tone. "Cliff, this puts a much different light on the war; this is, well this is an extraordinary find, this picture."

"You bet it puts a new light on things Frank, *and* on top of that, *they were faggots.* I fucking hate faggots, Frank."

Frank ended the call and laughed off-air while a commercial played, relieved that once again Kyle had caught the profanity before it made it on air. When he looked up and saw Kyle cracking up inside the glassed-in screener's booth, he knew Cliff's call would make its way into their list of favorites.

After the commercial break was nearly over, he rushed to inhale from his cigarette before setting it in the ashtray. He leaned toward the console, placed the headphones over his head and switched on his mic. From the corner of his eye, he could see Kyle counting down the seconds to airtime. Frank's readout indicated that Lucinda from Watts was on line one.

"Hello Lucinda from Watts, you had a run in with a shadow person?"

"Yeah hi Frank, it's not the first time, I've had a lotta run ins with these things, they ain't real people, real people have decency."

"Shadow people, for those of you listening who don't know, are remnants or particles of people, that materialize in the shape of shadows. They hide underneath things in an attempt to avoid detection."

"I just want mine to get out from under my bed. We can't… my husband and me can't have, you know, relations, *motherfuckers*, stick up their heads and watch us." Kyle's hand went up to assure Frank that Lucinda's motherfucker didn't get through.

"That's unusual, normally they're a fearful bunch, shadow people don't like to be looked at, seen, photographed or—"

"You mean take pictures or like taping? Because I'm sure as hell taping them mother-fuckers."

"Lucinda, this may be the problem." Frank said as he nodded a thank you towards Kyle, grateful to the kid for catching yet another cuss word.

"Oh they all huddled and shit under our bed…Frankly, we want them out, gone, adios. My husband's eyes have been roamin'… seen him looking at Ol' Char's *tits*….can't have that."

Frank glanced toward the glassed in screener's booth, slightly troubled to see Kyle holding up one finger, his forefinger, meaning he'd let one of Lucinda's cuss words through. Frank wondered if it'd been shit or tits, either way, he wouldn't know until later.

"Cameras of any sort frighten them, Lucinda. Don't try hiding it somewhere, either; just turn it off and put it away. They'll go soon enough."

Leaving the station after one in the morning was always odd for Frank. Few places were open so late, even in Hollywood. Prostitutes, johns short on cash, addicts of all kinds, serious drinkers and guys like him who had nowhere else to go frequented the few bars that were still open.

Matilda's Tavern was nearby and open. It was quiet and a good enough place to sit and have a few beers before heading home.

Once there, Frank headed straight for a stool at the empty bar, greeting Tim the bartender with a nod. When he sat, he liked to imagine the stressors of his shift suddenly becoming lighter than air, like tiny bits of lint coming loose off a coat. He did this while he waited for his first beer; it was the closest thing to meditation that he knew.

He drank his first beer slowly, allowing his thoughts to roam randomly. One trivial thought gave way to the next, while he enjoyed the soothing mumble of the few patrons—three men sat in a booth up front—and welcomed the lulling glow of the amber lamps that sat on the bar top.

One thing was wrong, though. Suddenly, as if swept in by a malicious breeze, a foul smell shook Frank from his reverie. From the corner of his eye, he made out the figure of a man sitting directly next to him. *How did he get so close without my noticing?*

He couldn't see him, but he could certainly smell the guy. His stench was a noxious mixture of dried piss, an alcoholic's stale breath ,and an onion-like body odor that always reminded Frank of chili. He had to look at the guy, but it wasn't curiosity that drove him to it, it was repulsion.

Without a word of prompting the man addressed Frank, "I'm John." The old man put out his hand and Frank shook it. "I don't usually come in on Thursdays."

"I'm Frank." Frank looked into the man's clear and almost pretty blue eyes, noting that he was older than he'd first thought.

John replied quickly saying, "I know who you are," causing Frank caution. The man's tone was hard to place. Was it disdain? Dismissal? Disapproval? *Fuck it,* he thought.

John took a gulp from his scotch before looking at Frank. "When I had a job, I'd head home after work, never here. "

"I see." Frank felt at a loss; he didn't know exactly how to respond, or if he really wanted to.

John shifted in his stool, then signaled Tim for another round, including Frank's glass in the gesture. John smiled big, leaned forward into the bar and placed his elbows on the glossy wood surface.

31

"I gave up drinking twenty-five years ago. I've been re-drinking for months now. Or has it been longer, Tim?"

Tim called out from the far end of the bar. "Keep me out of this."

"That's right, it's my fuck-up, my responsibility. Thanks for the reminder, Tim."

John looked down at the counter and then up into Frank's eyes. The next thing John said surprised him, not because of its content, but because of the blunt way he said it.

"Almost got on your show once." John held his gaze when he delivered this.

Frank nodded and pretended to take interest in his beer, turning the glass on the counter, anything to avoid the prick of the older man's eyes.

"I was on hold even, waiting for the guy who screens to come back." John grunted or guffawed, and looked like he was deep in thought.

Frank considered moving from the bar to get away from the guy, but there was a keen intelligence in the way John spoke that intrigued him. It was the one thing that caused him to stay. John was clearly an educated guy, maybe down on his luck—by the looks of his soiled clothing and his smell—but tons of brilliant guys messed up and lost jobs. There was darkness in this guy, though; what exactly it was, he couldn't say, but it was there.

"Most people do a lot of thinking when they're on hold. Don't you think, Frank?"

Frank nodded, before he looked up and met John's blue eyes half way.

"I had time to weigh all the things I wanted to say, when one question struck me." John laughed bitterly before he went on, "What the *fuck* was I hoping to get out of calling The Frank fuckin' Sound Show?"

John stopped laughing; his face grew solemn and drawn. Then he said, "Actually, that wasn't the question. The question I had would've troubled your audience."

It was at this point that Frank came close to leaving. It wasn't that John was being nasty, he wasn't—his tone was more regretful than angry—it was that Frank disliked talking about his show. It had grown tiresome over the years. There were two responses he got from people and they never varied. Hate being one, because there were people who hated the show. Those people always suggested he was an insensitive monster for egging crazy people on. The other reaction was love, because there were people who loved his show. He remembered a college kid who'd stopped him at a gas station who said, "Frank, dude, your show is insane, it's the funniest goddamn thing on the radio." Given time, he was sure John was headed one way or the other.

"Listen, John, I just got off air, and I don't know about you, but once I'm off—"

"I hung up when it struck me," John interrupted, "that the world forgives crazy people, like they do on your show, but they always condemn a guy like me. My problem is that I keep forgetting to accept, I forget to accept that my life stings."

"Stings? As in hurts?" Frank was trying to cut to the chase. "Well, fuck all of us then, because life hurts."

John kept on talking like he hadn't heard Frank's comment. "That night, the night I almost got on, you and some callers were talking about evil… of all things. But what bothered me, the thing that got me to pick up the phone, was that none of you talked about restraint."

Frank looked over at Tim, who held up a glass in place of asking if Frank wanted another. As soon as Frank nodded, Tim leaned into the tap and began to pour.

"No mention that some of us, maybe not you or the next guy," John gestured toward Tim who set Frank's beer down, "but some of us live a life of white-knuckle, grip-as-hard-as-you-can self-discipline."

Here was when Frank lost it. "You think you're the only one with demons, John?" Frank laughed, and maybe it came out sounding angrier than he'd intended, but he was tired.

Tim joined in; laughing with a vehemence Frank hadn't heard from him, "Shit, I'd trade all my demons for your one. In a second." Then he walked away, seemingly uninterested in further conversation.

John watched Tim's back, "If only it could be so easy. Would suck for the poor sap who got stuck with mine; hell, he may not have what it takes."

"Restraint isn't a virtue that's valued much anymore," added Frank.

John laughed in agreement, "You got that right. Remember the old Frankenstein movie?"

Frank drank from his drink and nodded.

"The first time I watched it, I saw *me*. That monster had no manner of not hurting. He was doomed from the start.

"He was a fuckin' monster, they're supposed to scare, maim and kill… hell, even little girls who offer them flowers get killed.

"That's right. I was just a boy when I first laid eyes on the monster, but I knew my impulses were just as incurable as his. Imagine being a little kid and already knowing your destiny included a lifetime of being misunderstood?"

Frank decided to allow the man his monologue, sensing that he was nearing an end, a final conclusion.

"No crazy doctor created me, but something did….even as a boy I wondered why god would bring evil into the world. Why bother?"

"John, everyone thinks they're misunderstood…"

They sat for a long time, Frank too absorbed in his thoughts to say any more. It occurred to him that John might be done, and he considered thanking him for the beer and heading home. All this went through his mind until he saw that John was leaning on the bar, his face buried in his folded arms, as if he'd fallen asleep.

But John hadn't fallen asleep, because Frank saw that his shoulders were shaking and that his ears and the side of his face were red. John was crying like a kid.

He didn't know what to do, so he put his hand on John's crouched shoulder, feeling the bones that couldn't be seen through the older man's coat and the sorrow that swelled through his body. These could be alcohol-fueled sobs, Frank suspected, but an instinct told him it was something else.

A mumble came up from John's huddled form, and then he raised his head and spoke, so Frank could hear.

"As God is my witness and as much as I've wanted to, I've never touched a child. There were times when I was left alone with a much too trusting parent, so many times I could have fed my monster.... I've carried my detestable load from the day I recognized it, and chose the sting instead. Could you imagine Frankenstein's monster opting for a life of loneliness? Denying himself the need to kill. Perhaps, killing to him came naturally as does my odious inclination."

It was then that Frank realized he'd removed his hand from the destitute man's shoulder. Just after John's first confession, he'd lifted his hand away in disgust. As startled as he was by the confession, he'd not expected his own intense revulsion. He'd sensed John had some dark shit in his closet, but not *that* dark. After years of radio he'd come to accept the darkness of others, but never had he been face to face with this type of...what? Monster?

Now he understood why John had hung up, why he'd not waited to go on air. Had he, Frank knew John's darkness, even if he'd never molested a child, would've been morally impossible for others to tolerate. Hell, he'd removed his own hand from the crying man's shoulder.

"Now, here is the question I would have posed to your listeners had I stayed on the line. Consider me, a fiend who chose to hurt in place of seeking out the only thing that made sense to me, because, if you need to know, being with children, makes total sense to a sick fuck like me."

John sniffled and it struck Frank as pitiful, a gesture meant only to attract pity. Then John gathered himself to finally ask, "Who would you say is the better man? The one undaunted by unpopular proclivities and who lives a sin free-life, or the one who struggles with one every minute of every day?"

Frank openly looked at John's profile, at the man's sharp long nose and considered the predicament, the question asked of him. A silence grew between the two men, forcing its way like an evolutionary safeguard that separated the good man from the one whose darkness was outside of human understanding. Frank had nothing to say; no words came to him.

Everything inside of Frank told him to get up and leave; in fact, he'd been struggling with that very desire to flee all night, and yet, he'd stayed.

Fight or flight, his old therapist had called it. Fight or flight. He'd chosen the right one at seven. When Reynolds, his dad's fishing buddy had pressed his hand over his pants and tried to squeeze his cock, he'd hollered and slammed on Rey's face. That time he'd chosen the right one.

He got up off his stool, and nodded toward Tim, who knew to put Frank's beers on his monthly tab. At the door, he turned and saw John, still sitting at the bar, staring out in front of him. The only thing there that Frank could see was the mirror behind the bar.

What did John see as he stared? Did he see Frankenstein, the pathetic, manmade creature plagued with an inability to control his impulses?

The sky was still dark when he walked outside. As he made his way to the car, Frank remembered the first time he'd seen the Frankenstein movie. He remembered the black and white horror of the film, the eerie beauty of the fictional town, the frantic reaction of the frightened villagers, and the uncomfortable pity he'd felt for the creature. The compassion he'd felt for the monster had seemed more grotesque to him, than the monster itself.

He'd been young, too, probably just a kid, when he'd first seen the movie. He remembered sitting alone on the bare living room floor, his dried-out half-eaten bowl of Capt'n Crunch sitting next to him. The sound of a neighbor's lawn mower humming not too far off and how relieved he'd been to hear it. The lawn mower, just like the Miller's barking dog, were reminders of things mundane and normal, things that put a wedge between him and the terrifying world of the monster.

UNSOUND
~ Kelley Jean White

I took you
from the shadow of the mountain
dust caking
your milky skin

between two lakes
and the rock's high anger
to green, I thought,
and a village peace

but you saw hurt
where I saw beauty
in the great gee ox
and his knobbled knees

you lived with horses
before they broke you
showed the withered haunch
the crippled calf

the empty barn
dust on hay moldering
the yoke too heavy
choked by burning steel

APOCALYPTIC GODIVA
~ Walter Bargen

The weather leaves a depression in the bed,
a storm of sheets and blankets.
The bruised tower of pillows,
cumulus at one end of the stained mattress
Headboard stretches to the horizon. That won't
go away and can't be reached Walls of fog
press in. She lies there forecasting faces.
In this new life they do whatever she wants
except call for help. From this angle,
staring over the bed's edge, the floor is her ceiling.
She can't raise her hand to wave hello
or move her head to look up.
One foot free and with her big toe, she reaches
the night table and punches automatic redial.
The police break the chain latch, unlock
the bedroom door. The paramedics find her
in bed, stroke victim who woke
twisted as a bolt of lightning. They hear
the hungry dog curled in the debris
of the kitchen. The steel moons of stethoscopes
swing from their necks. They can't lift
her universe or roll her easily. With scissors
they cut away her gown, then she's free to panic,
to stand, to walk the hall. No stroke of luck,
weathering the sweet tooth of loneliness: Mars,
Butterfingers, Mounds, unwrapped, half-eaten,
rolled thickly in the sheets, melted against her body,
and hardened in the morning of an unheated room.
No downpour, tornado, Force Ten gale needed
to shake her, but scissored free of this sweet apocalypse.

"radius"

~ devin wayne davis

watching her
& him, you have beautiful—
if disillusioned—blue-green
eyes;
i want to see
your silver tears
catch them.

MAD SONG
~ Edward Butscher

I nightmare cream walls
in breasts
female
hemispheres at their lull
at rest, milked
of small skulls.
A scream in the background
always
female
as the boneless sapling
shedding faces
in a sudden Fall.
Now it has sifted inside
harder
female
as urgent lily bulbs
cracking
icebox ribs
hearts of lovers and dead aunts
blossoming
out loud
from the aria I scale
when Spring
gives commands:
stand straight
shut the light
open wide.

DREAM IN THE AFTERNOON
~ Edward Butscher

A small ball of auburn dog
on a shelf that does not exist
in the bedroom no longer mine
too near the ocean's tolling din
like a porcupine pup but fluffy
luminous as an illustration
recollected from childhood
I gently cradle and carry
into the restored farm kitchen
where furious women and girls
materialize out of air and mind:
Amy alive among them, doll in
hand and desperate to be saved
Aunt Olga glaring in a teenager's
glossy red and green raincoat
the crowd of them multiplying
around us as they condemn me
without ceasing their chores
Amy's panicky hold on my arm
knocked loose by their bony
bodies' pinball batterings.
The dog could be that papillon
the old widow loved to parade
when I walked luncheonette
planks after school and football
or a fabulous bestiary notion
imported from medieval France
except for those round brown
disturbingly familiar eyes and
flick of a quiver as I lift her
free of the raging female torrent
like the baby rabbit the cats

41

chased inside for me to rescue
and release in a nearby wood
the summer both my parents died
only noticing the dried blood
on my hands at the dinner table
after the enormous seashore sky
had swooped down with darkness
to sweep away the huge fir trees
hugging this house to earth.

CANDLELIGHT DINNER
~ Fraida Liba Levine

evening crumples around him
all wrinkled and distracted,
like the sandwich folded in dull foil paper
at the end of a day.
hungry, like that
for all of It.
the last of the sunlight gleams in the paint of his pickup
it smells mortal,
like the hair singed by his blowtorch.

INVASIVE PROCEDURES
~ Fred Ferraris

She crossed the border with fear and trembling, a person without a passport, and entered a rapidly mutating realm of indefinite music, dangerous songs. You invited this fatherless symmetry into your home, and you understand, with a sympathy almost like anguish, the complacent distance that separates the man from the woman. She packed up her hopes, put a rose in her hair, and offered herself to the future, but she may have misread the future's intentions. Warning: metaphors are like unto sand. Homemade rockets, a world view in shambles, a world view skewed by funky geography. The white hunter's house is built out of wind. But he doesn't know wind from stone. His faith stands firm. I study him behind his iron gate that delineates his eternal imprisonment. At the same time the woman has begun, not without ostentation, the methodical study of Farsi. In her world, vowels will balance out. I don't mean there isn't a suicidal beauty in her. Or a cobra-infested labyrinth. Any day now, uninvited guests will commandeer her home. In a few years she will be attending tedious lectures delivered in dialect. Then she will be convicted of having a gap in her memory. Even so, her posture and manner will remain the same, that is to say, habitual. History, that string of bloodied pearls, will be honored to say, It's a beautiful morning, get out your guns. I myself have fallen into a slot machine, and I am expecting guests.

Imagine for a moment that you are a platform-sweeper in an abandoned railway station. Robot skulls leer in rocket's red glare. Tracer bullets shower down like meteorites, light fixtures shatter, and it occurs to you that this might be a good time to get out of town for a century or two. A train pulls into the station, the roof collapses, the station departs without you. You'd like to turn your proto-romantic vision into a platform you can stand on, but a small oscillation in perception could signal a quick goodbye.

A gangster chieftain, his anomolous mistress, their faces painted lurid with moral cosmetics. He claims that peace is coming soon, darkness hides inside her smile. But the bamboozler's spiel is a peripheral indignity. His narrow back-alley rhetoric makes you want to slap him silly, but wait a moment, I'm expecting a guest. Her invitation was delivered in a legal-size coffin. I hope she brings some reading matter in her tote bag of hopes to remind me of how I got here. These days anyone can be his own third-rate online travel agent, but remembering where we used to be takes more serious effort. Night tears through the station. Up on the platform the white hunter is speaking in a dialect that comes with an army and a navy. I wonder if my guest carries a weapon of her own? The doorbell rings. A cobra dances, the surge of life, then a moan. Tomorrow is buried in yesterday's grave. Dead skin, old bones. The doorbell rings. I fix my smile. Here she is, with a rose in her hair.

Low Coherences
~ Fred Ferraris

> "A white hunter is nearly crazy."
> —Gertrude Stein, *Tender Buttons*

The blue-violet flame in the white hunter's eye braises the brisket of his obsolescence, stirs advantage into his tea, his posey philosophy like a Gyro Gearloose contraption, its pale blue light bathing the busted Ferris wheel at the edge of a drowning city. A tingling in his prick tells him that his voice is being broadcast into back alleys where his thoughts aren't worth a hill of beans. Jesaru Durango reviews the Oracle's prognosis, lays the page aside. The white hunter studies his disconnected head, amazed at the snakes nested under its tongue.

Jesaru makes a courtesy call, throws questions of justice into a blender, unleashes a fusillade of gunpowder teas. He likes to work back alleys. He has visions of tragicomic futures, but he doesn't know what they mean. A young girl dressed in blue suede brocade stirs her tea with a bloody knuckle; a small boy armed with boar tusks and gourd saws searches for saviors among the spear men.

Jesaru Durango sleeps with snake fangs under his pillow. He makes his bed with awe. He suspects the Oracle knows something, but the Oracle isn't talking. Jesaru has received a message from his short-term memory and who knows what that means? A body is not a book, a mounted head yields no small profit, her position is well-known, his position is mismanaged—why a man without a head must wait until the cobras are fed.

The white hunter is a professional whose intellectual methods are clothed in Teutonic regalia, a pugnacious profiteer, a man of pervasive jerky habits, a Lollapalooza in lamasery drag. Only you know what that means. A small girl betrayed by arthritic hands, a poem pried from a listing wheel, a fleshy calyx swollen with badge-men. At times it's difficult to tell a white hunter's tongue from a speak-your-weight machine.

The indigo flame in Jesaru's eye toasts the riddle of the maladroit hunter. He tossed a burial plot and tumbled onto a rosy larynx. That was before the tongue repressors crashed the Garden of Bodiless Noggins.

A pale blue flame bathes Jesaru Durango in nitroglycerine light. The white hunter raises a hill of beans. The citizens distract themselves with flashing colored neon, or a small boy stumbles into the path of an oncoming Sputnik.

The present situation would like to entrance you, but you've already eyeballed the exit. People are saying the white hunter had an audience with the Oracle and shot holes through her falcon's hood. By the time you sense the presence of someone and awake, the spear men are on you like fleas. People are saying Jesaru Durango has cornered the market on blue suede brocade. He claims he survived the hard times on a stew of boar spew and silage. He likes his prochronic visions seasoned with tectonic legato.

And aboard the Sputnik a riddled hawk, snakes without fangs, defoliated trees. "Do I know what I know?" Jesaru asked. "Not ahead of your time," the Oracle answered.

We had no choice but to banish the bitch. The Empire no longer tolerates troublesome or quarrelsome persons. Jesaru Durango keeps to himself, polishes his tusk with honking nitro. Even here at the edge of the drowned city we can hear the hunter clearing his throat. But in these back alleys no one listens. We've already heard what the man has to say. He is, after all, our white hunter.

He is, after all, one of us.

BRACELET
~ Gunta Krasts Voutyras

The piece of jewelry was filigree, made of copper and dipped in gold. Very fine work, precise and delicate. This bracelet wrapped in brown paper had traveled in the pocket of a man who had walked many months. His feet wrapped in rags. Boots without soles. Only tops. Walking hundreds of miles. Looking for his family.

He was coming from a labor camp deep in the Italian Alps. From digging trenches. At times digging graves for those who were no longer alive in the morning at the yell of "Aufsteigen." Same unfortunates he shared the barracks with.

It was soul-wrenching. The brutality. The horrible food. Hot water with rotten potatoes. If a guard did not like a laborer he got no potato. Just hot water with no salt. No one could exist on this. Many men died.

The man held on. He occupied his mind with thoughts of his two little girls. Of his wife. Of his flower garden. The pear trees planted just the year before. The colorful dahlias growing along a tall fence. Rows and rows of potatoes planted last spring. All planted with care. Nurtured with love. All for the future and his family. Thoughts of educating his girls at the university. Remembrances of conducting dinner at his dining room table surrounded by friends and family.

All that is gone now. The large comfortable house destroyed. The gardens neglected. Destruction from bombs falling all night, every night. His children most likely spending their nights in an underground shelter he himself had dug in the middle of his potato field. Work of two generations destroyed. All life altered into the unknown, seemingly hopeless future.

During the many inhuman hours spent digging trenches he understood that a human being without hope is as good as dead. One must never give up. One must fight on with one's last breath. The greatest tool against tyranny, mind control, brutality and all other forms of terror we humans are so good at inflicting on each other is the ability to not lose faith and sustain one's spirit.

One early spring morning the gate to the labor camp was found to be wide open without a Nazi in sight. All those who could walk, crawl or hobble left the camp. Some to the surrounding villages. Looking for food. Some looking for work. Others just putting distance between the camp and themselves.

My father, feet wrapped in rags, made his way to the nearest village. He helped a local farmer resurrect his vineyard. As payment the man asked him to choose a piece of jewelry out of a hand-carved box. Dad chose a delicate, narrow bracelet. Next morning he took the only road out of town. In his pocket, wrapped in brown paper, rested the bracelet. In his heart, hope and faith he will find his family.

TO BE
~ Yvette A Schnoeker-Shorb

I am light on the wind
wailing over water. I am
an original daughter cell
of some primitive form
related to you. I am
explosive
like seeds bursting
from the pod of a weed,
like hidden potential
of misplaced genes
on a chromosome. I am
these words compelled
to write themselves real
so you will notice

                              I am.

FRAGMENTS
~ Tree Riesener

No longer scrutineer nor even explainer, through the long hot mornings of summer I read old Japanese paperbacks, the paper so yellow and brittle I have to turn the pages with great care, comforted by the moral struggle, endured through seasons of heroic silence, as to whether a woman should wear one more or less under-kimono, with death the penalty for the wrong choice.

People do die for trivia. I have always known this.

From the Latin. Trivium. A place where three roads meet—the perfect opportunity to exchange stories, gossip, information. Where you learn methods for things to do and things not to do.

So small, the things we die for. Kill for. Fragments.

If you talk to murderers, the motive is not usually anything grand, like "We could not agree on the filioque clause in the Nicene Creed—does the Holy Spirit proceed from the Father and the Son, or do both the Son and the Spirit proceed from the Father?"

No, it's usually for something like the way, twenty times a day, she says "A penny for your thoughts" or the way he wipes his mouth after eating a fried egg.

Like old colonial explorers in Africa who put on formal dress each evening in their huts, I know how easy it would be for me to slide into lassitude, so I keep working hours, get up on time, drink coffee and dress before beginning my reading.

On Saturday mornings, I wear my bathrobe, leave my novels and watch samurai movies on cable, walking off into the sunset with that lonely blind figure who lazes around for days and then, finally one day, galvanized into action by some cue obviously unexplainable by sub-titles, kills forty people in batches of ten at a time, seemingly for looking too directly at the delicate daughter of the impoverished landowner as she drifts through the frames with downcast eyes, occasionally kneeling to serve tea.

But since he is blind, how does he know about this? Does someone tell him at the crossroads?

When you do not see, how do you know there is danger?

Sunday after lunch is the Bollywood festival, reminding me that the *danse macabre* goes on. I have a favorite, obviously popular since it is repeated often, of terrorists bursting into song and dance as they go through the aisle of the airplane, with a soulful solo by the handsome head terrorist singing of his regret at never seeing his sweetheart again, until the camera zooms in on a close-up of the girl, who has disguised herself with horn-rimmed glasses and hair pulled back into a librarian's bun, to die with her sweetheart as the plane goes down in flames.

Once she whips her glasses off and slips a burqa over her head, he recognizes her and their swan song begins.

Is it worth noting that the passengers, after initial apprehension, are so won over by this Romeo and Juliet spectacle that they join in the chorus?

After the crash, the head terrorist and his sweetheart are seen in the sky surrounded by the benevolent, beaming passengers. Everything has been forgiven. The terrorists and the terrorized have arrived at some sort of *rapprochement*, formed a blended family, and are living happily in a heavenly afterlife. No wonder it is a popular movie.

On Sunday afternoons, I sit on the sunny terrace in my bathrobe with limey gin and work on my summer's goal—devising, with twenty-six letters, inspired by the monkey with a typewriter legend, a second complete poem by Sappho, to add to the one that survives. I keep my pen in a pocket so I can write with ink my body's heat has warmed.

During spring, I had taken the single surviving line out of the legendary four volumes by Cornelius Gallus, friend of Vergil, and remembered one of his lost elegies to love. When it was too casually received, I burned it, and used the ashes to trace a heart on my forehead on Valentine's Day.

I am a mender of sweaters, riveter of old china, saver of the broken. There is nothing that cannot be mended except when it is smashed into bits.

Even then it can be mosaic. Each phoenix that rises from the ashes is a different bird. I consider fragments.

The radio tells me that abortion was responsible for the crime rate dropping in half, the first generation culled by legalized abortion grew up to be more lawful teenagers than the last generation.

Before or after they were told?

The water supply is so full of Zoloft, Prozac and Xanax that our bloodstreams have become biological hazards from satisfying our thirst. Can we take Rappacini's daughter as our model?

Princess Diana, descended from the Merovingians and so from Jesus and Mary Magdalene, was murdered in the Pont l'Alma tunnel, which in pre-Christian times was a sacrificial site, to send a signal that Saint Diana, a new form of the triple moon goddess Diana, would imminently return to dethrone the usurping Windsors.

"Where is her jewelry?" the queen asked.

You may say these fragments will not make a satisfying mosaic.

Anything will make a mosaic. Come with me.

The abortion survivors, eager not to become murder victims, keep themselves well hydrated and are thus able to cope, even though the water is lobotomizing. In time, they organize package trips to the lonely island tomb of Diana, in her role as the triple moon goddess.

Or

Diana, in her role as the triple moon goddess, baptizes. with the magical water of tranquility and forgetfulness. all the traumatized abortion survivors who come to her lonely island tomb. They grow halos that look like crowns and the tomb site becomes known as the Island of Light.

Or

The abortion survivors learn of their destroyed cohort, and even as the dead of World War I came back as the lost of James Dean's generation, undergo surgery to become Dianas, although not triple moon goddesses, and devise colorful cocktails of the lethal water of forgetfulness.

You see?

We all have our reasons. Most seem trivial to others. A throne, traces of egg yolk.

I wish I had waited for a grander reason.

Use these to make a mosaic.

According to Herodotus, the Scythians of the fifth century B.C. threw hemp on heated stones and then inhaled, becoming more and more intoxicated until finally they jumped up and started dancing and singing. The Old Testament recipe for Jesus' anointing oil required twelve pounds of cannabis.

This is what I think. Considering what was waiting for him, I am happy to think of Jesus high.

Would you choose the prophet Jeremiah or Hosea to make a music video of your life?

This is what I think. If the song was about aching unrequited love, I'd choose Hosea, who sacrificed all to marry a temple hooker. But for apocalypse and total damn-all of every kind, you can hardly do better than Jeremiah.

Only three knights were allowed to see the Grail—Bors, Perceval and Galahad, because they were pure at heart.

This what I think. All the women saw it. Handled it. Used it.

After it appeared in my friend Helen's kitchen, she kept it on the counter for a long time. It got filled up with rubber bands, recipe cards, snapshots of her kids when they were babies—the kind of stuff any non-utilitarian object in a kitchen tends to accumulate.

She gave it to me the first year I was alone, when she saw me through the window at twilight, lighting the candles on my cake.

I use it for my gin and tonic as I read Japanese novels on the sunny terrace.

For all of recorded history, we have looked for a few hours of respite. Even God sometimes needs sweet dreams and music, soft through the night, from neither the tormented nor the psychotic. The Holy Grail is different things to different people. A gin and tonic, plus music, plus the sweet incense of forgetulness will always help you make it through the night.

Use them, these fragments.

Can you sin in a dream? What if you dream sin all the time and you confess until the priest grows distant and says you can't come any more?

Hail, Mary, I am very tired. Pray for me, now and at the hour of my death.

When the novels are finished and the last movie watched, make my coffin of boards at which the poor have eaten.

Fragments.

LATE SNOW
~ Peter S Lee

Ilene ran her hands through hair as thick and black as coal dust. It fell around her shoulders in the white linen moon. The frost-covered trees were like so many strong, young men, standing there to court her. They were standing in a wonderland of newly fallen snow.

The silence was the silence that descends upon strangers who have traveled all night in the pouring rain. It was the silence that converges with darkness in prayer. The houses strung along the hills were like the lights on a Christmas tree. Ilene lay down and spread her wings to make an angel in the snow.

She watched the sky for angels, softly ringing, to appear. She waited for a sign. But all she saw was a shooting star, illuminated by the moon. The bright white gown of taffeta, blowing in the wind, swept the contours of a face cloaked in frozen tears.

She had tried to bridge the gap between love and money. But there is no accounting for the customs of the rich. In his own way, in his dedication to his work, Martin had transcended the money. But even his intelligence could not trump the pull of blood.

The wedding had been a contrast between the haves and the have-nots. Her attempts to unite the families had been a disaster. She was Pittsburgh Lutheran and he was Eastern European snob. But none of this compared to Leo having come.

When he touched her on the arm to dance, she fainted. She came to looking up into his eyes. She realized as she danced with him that he was whom she should have married. She realized that Martin was just a child.

It was a quiet, quiet house. Martin slept before the fire. Ilene sat in her wedding dress and drank a cup of tea. As she stared into the fire, she heard chimes, ringing loudly. There was no explanation for the mystery.

When the ringing stopped, all that she could hear was Martin. He seemed to fill the house with noise. His kind were loud, even while sleeping. It was a bleating kind of snore.

As God was her witness, she had tried. But they spoke a language all their own. From under half-closed eyelids, they viewed the world with disapprobation. The patterns of their lives were marked by deep self-interest.

Ilene took off her wedding dress and hung it on a beam. It hung like a ghost in the firelight. She danced with the fairies in faded blue jeans. She combed her long, dark hair.

Our lives are spent traveling from the darkness to the light, compressed and bound in a world of cares. We stop at intervals to rest, or to hide, in places that no one knows, until we are too tangled to take flight or too unraveled to dare.

Ilene looked down at his sleeping face. It was the face of a man with no secrets to reveal. Ilene was the light of his life. But she felt just like a chair. She was something for him to sit on, a depository, an ending to his day. This was why she had to leave.

The light through the trees was golden yellow brown and the sky was filled with sparrows. Ilene followed the flight of a chimney swift, swooping near to the ground. The snow gave off a crunching sound when rolled over by the tires. It was a frozen esplanade, which she drove through down the mountain.

SHORE
~ Larissa Shmailo

It will continue, he says,
even when the water breaks white,
even when the surface currents seem
to be going the wrong way.

The river, I tell him, is grey, and the ocean is for others.

I have crossed the river on stones and planks,
while others swam, inviting me in
and I dove just to please them, pretending
I could swim too.

My path is broken; the white caps are hard
there are too many gaps, always

I must find the connector: I use wire and wood
and rusty nails, these broken rafts,
whatever it takes to cross.

I don't know tides or currents,
have never understood how the river flowed;
perhaps it does not.

There is only the leap, and my heart in my mouth:
I can't walk this hard water or swim,
and I will never see land.

I will be your dolphin, he says,
and you will not drown.

How can I explain that
I am not afraid of drowning:

I have drowned many times, come up,
gasping for air, and dead, many times
what it is that
I can't swim
and the water is hard.

It will continue, he says
even when the surface currents
seem to be going the wrong way.

MAPPING
~ Larissa Shmailo

The pigeons fly in cursive flocks, graceful arcs
Except this one, gone ahead or left behind, in urgent solo flight.
Below a willow leans, thin and sparse, looking for sparks,
Like an addict in the morning's trafficked street.
A man like you hands me a urine cup, and sleeps.

I have told you before, here at the doorway
Of a thousand unhappy homes: there is something more
Of place than time or space in loneliness. Come,
Reluctantly spend the day. Look at the unconnected stars,
The uncollected lights without name or home or
Constellation of their own, and imagine a use with me
For all that doesn't fit.

SLATE
~ Craig Saunders

Even the snow flouts the rules this morning. It is supposed to float and swirl. It doesn't. It falls flat and dead, landing heavily on the veranda.

Icicles hang from the guttering above me. The house looks like it has teeth. I blow smoke hard into the still air and the house is a dragon snoring.

I pull up my collar and cup my second Marlboro of the morning between pink hands. I never got the hang of smoking with gloves on.

The veranda creaks, but only for me. It wouldn't wake her. It is subdued, a forlorn farewell. The snow holds the sound down, gently restraining the sounds from within. The snow, my ally.

Tomas Moran comes to his window in the house opposite, pulling the curtains apart to see outside. He waves, and shrugs, then closes the curtains on the outside again. I can barely see him through the growing, silent, storm. It is a wonder he is able to see me. I wear grey today, and there is a full hundred yards between us. But perhaps, as is fitting, the snow allows us one final wave, no closer than we ever had been, from across the chasm that separates our two houses. It could have been a gulf, or an ocean. It does not matter to me that he sees me. Soon, I will be gone. Who cares for goodbyes?

Had it been raining, it would have thundered on the veranda roof. Even then it wouldn't wake her.

The coffee is already going cold. The third cup bubbles noisily behind me. Snow muffle obviously isn't omni-directional.

What a time to leave. January blizzards cutting off the main drag, cars still slewed, now abandoned, cluttering Matherson Avenue. A proud old tree has already fallen to the blight.

Ice cracks somewhere overhead.

Snow looks after its own.

I am cold, but not on the outside. I think it will let me pass.

No one is out on the street today. Cars are piled so high with fluff that they look more like random hills, peppering the streets.

Ancient barrows of blighted England, wights hiding in the darkness underneath, their wails covered by the silent doorman. Yesterday's old snowmen sit in front gardens, bouncing for porches. The snow lets the children out, just not the adults. Children's souls aren't generally tainted.

Here I am, all alone, looking at the icy slate covering the road, the hard cold death awaiting the unsuspecting as the snow comes in to cover it.

I am cold.

I am one of its own.

Smoke swirls for an instant and an unheard hiss I know is there signals its death. I stand for a moment.

I try to keep quiet as I shut the door gently behind me. My third cup is in my hand, with my third cigarette. Her face comes to me. The coffee percolator gives a dry steam rasp and goes quiet.

I rub some life into my hands and run my fingers through my hair. I smoke another cigarette. The flame sputters in the cold.

Yesterday I had given up smoking. I didn't know it was to be our last day together. Early that morning we had eaten waffles together. We spent the day inside, knowing that outside was for children and children alone. It had been the perfect day. A Saturday spent snug and warm with gentle trickles of sludgy pre-snow beginning to turn into real snow, huge, almost warm, flakes, settling in the street, on people's front lawns, in the road. The cars that came down the street crept, as if trying not to wake the street from its winter slumber.

We had lain in bed for the rest of the morning, both with heads propped on pillows, staring out at the gathering storm. The wind was strong and silent then, the children coming out to play, their cries of delight muffled in mufflers. Mittens on their hands were caked in snow. They rolled and tumbled and made angels. As the storm grew stronger, whiter, the snowmen evolved from the earth, little balls into big, one atop the other. Carrots for noses pilfered from warm and cozy kitchens.

I got up at midday and made us a lunch of chicken soup and hot fresh bread from the oven. She had stayed in bed, waiting for my return. While the soup bubbled gently behind me I stood at the kitchen door, looking out. The snow gathered strength as the soup cooked. The smell of roasting bread came from the oven. I got a tray down from the top cupboard.

Back in bed, we watched the snow again.

She never left the house. That perfect Saturday I was happy to stay in, too. Most days I left her alone in the house. I don't know what she did all day, except to say I know she never left. There was nothing for me to worry about while I left. She would stay safe indoors.

The icicles above my head crackled and brought me from my reverie. I lit another cigarette and drank some still steaming coffee from the mug. I held the coffee one handed and took a long drag on the cigarette. It was cold out here. I should put a coat on. My sweater kept out the worst, though. At least the cold that was outside.

I don't know why I'm dallying. I am cold. It will let me in. I know it.

I stare into the softly falling snowflakes and a sudden breeze swirls the snow around me. The snow falls onto my hands and into my coffee. Its death is sudden. The snow changes and leaves watery freckles on my skin.

That Saturday afternoon had been wonderful. We had made love. It was our first time. She was strange about closeness. In all the time we had known each other she had never given her body up to me. Under the covers, the heat from the radiator insufficient to warm her cold skin, we had embraced.

It was the first time and the last. It was wonderful. I savored it now. The remembrance of the touch. The cool, sheer feel of her skin. The creamy smoothness. I had been good. She had been better. Together it had been perfect. The perfect prelude to the perfect Sunday.

Today should have been perfect.

I should have let her sleep.

I let her sleep now and finished my coffee. I should go soon. She would wake if I made a sound. If I broke the silence of the snow the spell would be broken. I would lose all that I'd had that day. The remembered day. I would remember it forever. That first day. That last day.

Upstairs, she waits to be woken up. But she's cold, too. I'm not the only one. Sometimes you have to bring people into your world. Sometimes it's lonely being cold all on your own.

I close the door behind me and flip the latch. I laugh at myself—how considerate I am now of her agoraphobia. I unflip the latch.

I put the mug down and my cigarettes into my pocket.

I leave the door a little open and the wind bangs the shutter door behind me as I leave. I wrap my arms around myself and walk out into the cold. I am cold and we are all alone.

MINOTAUR
~ John Sweet

in the end
i say nothing

walk down this empty street instead
into the face of pale broken sunlight with
the lesser bones of priests ground
into fine powder beneath my feet

with the mother of my children
begging god for forgiveness

empty sounds from a bleeding mouth
empty hands cut off at the wrists
because the idea of war cannot be
considered w/out the idea of pain

the forest is where you run
only after all of
the cities have burned

being lost is what comes
after being alive

in the field of broken crosses
~ John Sweet

Had a baby born of rape, had a
gun, and she said she loved him,
and he said nothing at all.

Told the story until it
became a myth.

Cursed the walls, cursed the water,
stood naked at its edge until
it ran red with blood.

Held him close, and he wept.

Held him closer, and he screamed.

Sounded like a child waking up
in a room on fire.

HAND REACHING FOR GLASS AT 3 A.M.
~ Ronda Broatch

The child clamors for drink,
cracks the vessel of sleep.

> The rain wants in,
> while the window, indifferent,

knows no thirst.
A shell, upturned, cups

> ocean to its ear. Empty
> it speaks of rejection.

One face of glass beads sweat,
the other denies water's existence.

> The tongue speaks for the parched body.
> (Breath cleaves to breath.)

The hand divines water in darkness,
opens dreams.

> Sleep rubs against itself
> and anxiety is born.

How sleep cleaves to sleep,
then peels away.

> Mother and child,
> skin of bark. These too,

(if woven tightly)

                    hold water.

HE FORDS MY MIDNIGHT RIVER
~ Ronda Broatch

    I dreamt a man
with honeyed tongue
his eyes darker than truth

    the thin tree of his bones
cinched with desert
    feet rooted in river

    hands branched wide
under a changing sky.
    Later awake

    I wandered
into the arms of a surrogate
        church, found myself

    standing in the midst
        of a babbling homily.
I waded through fish

to the front row pew
into a current of blessings, dove in.
        I was gasping for breath

—the face on the plate looked
    so very like bread.
It seemed

no one noticed, save the priest
who fished me
    with her gaze

and thumbed a cross
    above my temple
    with a cool wet hand.

HER GARMENT BECOMES A LUMINOUS BODY
~ Ronda Broatch

    It hangs in the universe
of her wardrobe, bone-white
Tencel edged in nebulous
      midnight. It is

    a body awaiting the pressing
voyage of the *Rowenta*
Powerglide. Slide inside

    map the steaming terrain
for snaps and pockets. Traveler, follow
    the valley midland,
        dividing mountains

        study the time-lapse
   strip of moons eclipsed
by a wrinkle—

    see two already slip
through black holes, vanish
    to the dark side
       of the room.

BALD EAGLE VALLEY
~ Lisa Harris

People knew stars first, before they knew planets. Then they knew words. Finally, they knew the music the words made. They knew that when all three collided they found God. In pieces. And many of them believed if they could assemble the pieces correctly, they would be able to place themselves closer to God and grace.

Abbey had kept God tied up in her scarves in one of her dresser drawers for her entire life. Other people thought God resided under the tombstones in darkness. Abbey's ancestors tried to build God into their violins, making it so others could let God loose when they drew the bow across the strings.

Ezra, like Saint Thomas believed God could be found under a stone. He'd say to Eliza, "Split a stick and you'll find Jesus; lift a stone and you'll find God." At first Eliza believed him. Then she saw an eagle soaring above the Susquehanna in Bald Eagle Valley and in that instant, she knew God was in the air, holding the eagle aloft. She felt God in the fireplace when the coals glowed blue, and she heard God in the breaking branches of the pines during high winds. And at night she knew God watched her through the stars, that the millions of stars were God's eyes.

< >

The Yarnell Road twisted in front of the farmhouse where the Schnables lived in the shadows of the Allegheny Mountains. It led away from the hilltop, down into the hollows, and ended at the cemetery. For several hundred years, the Schnables had been walking that road with each other, with the Delaware, and alone. Season to season. Day and night.

Sometimes Abbey took her niece Eliza with her for walks during the daylight hours. Other times Abbey went to sit on a rock near the oldest graves where she wrote in her notebook about her ancestors. She wrote about her great-grandparents who made violins in Germany, marking each completed one with the first three letters of their name

"S H C"—Schnable. In America, they dropped the "C" for a while and began marking the violins they made in the new country with "S H"—as if the violin's true purpose was to calm those who played it and those who listened. She went to the graveyard for other reasons, too, but she didn't talk about those and she didn't write these secrets down.

Abbey had one of the violins marked with "S H"—the one that belonged to her grandfather and Eliza's great-grandfather. He was the first and only family member to play one. He called it a fiddle and played it boldly after he returned from his day in the potato fields. He played it on his wraparound porch where he sat swigging hard cider. He kept his jug hidden under the bench where it waited for him to return after he had spent his day hoeing potatoes, beating back the jewelweed and burdock. His wife, Nan, didn't allow secrets. She watched the world that closely, and when the air became filled with his fiddle music, she knew his gut was full of cider. So she bolted the door on him, vexed by his wild spirit, and left him to sleep in the hay. "You ain't nothing but an old, worn-out tomcat." Nan yelled at him from behind the closed door.

The Schnables are not Eliza and Abbey's only ancestors, but Schnable is the name most people remember in the valley and on the mountaintop. They remember Scottish Joneses, too, and running deep in both these families is a vein of willfulness, the kind that has helped them survive famine, guns, births, and the politics of life. This particular ancestry has been reduced to the acronym WASP, which trivializes it even as it suggests the ability within this group to sting.

The Jones family left Scotland where it touches northern England in 1642, and they sailed to Massachusetts carrying their clothes and two spinning wheels. It was a good time for Protestants to depart because of their persecution by the Crown, and especially good for the Joneses, who were hopelessly in debt and were as hungry as they had ever been, but they had hidden pieces of gold away so they could afford the passage. They and their seven children left on a foggy morning in March of that year: the sun, a thin slippery rim of tired yellow, and the shore, a zigzag of gray.

The Schnables walked away from their cottage in the German forest with their heads bowed, after burying three of their four children, all dead from a pox. They packed their violin-making tools with care. They did not look back. Each parent took a turn holding their oldest and only surviving son's hand, putting one foot down and then the other, one foot down and then the other, as they moved into the future. The boat that brought them arrived in Philadelphia on September 17, 1862. The date is recorded in their frayed Bible, along with all their children's names, birthdates and deaths. They arrived during the Civil War and settled in Yarnell, about two hours north of Harrisburg where Robert E. Lee and his army were headed when they got sidetracked to Gettysburg.

< >

Eliza's preoccupation with the Civil War grew directly out of her father's interest in it. He read her facts about the events leading up to the Battle of Gettysburg and what happened as a result. "It's an honor that we live in the state where the tide of that war got turned, Eliza," he'd say. He also read her Russian fairy tales with Baba Yaga stirring her cauldron. When she simply would not leave her dad alone, he'd read her articles about strip mining and its effect upon the land and water, until she fell asleep on the couch. Eliza would listen to anything just to be close to him, just as long as she could sit on his lap or beside him on the couch. That's how much she loved him. Another time when she was older, he told her about the Battle of Gettysburg. "You know, Robert E. Lee wanted Harrisburg because of its railroads. He had to plot and plan to get the cornfields between him and Harrisburg in order to secure a central railroad location, but he failed. Gettysburg was not planned, Eliza, but now everyone remembers it."

"Being remembered is important, isn't it, Daddy?"

"Oh yes, Eliza—it's important for people and places. You have to remember the facts and the feelings. You have to use your memory the same way you use your muscles. There were other important battles, too—like Antietam in Maryland. That one happened on the same day your ancestors landed in this country from Germany."

"Is this the story about—"

"Yes, it's the story. Antietam is seventeen miles from Harper's Ferry and the battle happened on September 17, 1862. It was the bloodiest one-day battle of the War—24,000 dead men. The battlefield was seventeen acres. Seventeen acres, seventeen miles, September 17—the day the Schnables arrived in Philadelphia. If they had known of the battle, they might have rushed to join it, or they might have gotten back on the boat—knowing what they knew about signs—they would not have been able to ignore all those seventeens!"

At this point, Ezra got out one of his Civil War books and found an old photo, "See all these dead men, Eliza—killing each other because of the differences in what they believed. You don't seen any of their faces—but, look, six hands, a raised knee, entangled bodies—seventeen bodies."

And Ezra took hold of Eliza's pointer finger and held it to the photo while they counted the seventeen bodies—one by one.

Eliza saw a split rail fence, four rails high, and a road off the left.

"Where's that road go, Daddy?"

"Off to Harrisburg if traveled north. That's the direction the Schnables went, until they reached the Bald Eagle Valley at the very center of Pennsylvania, setting their future and ours on this path."

< >

Julia Margery Jones was born in a one-room house with a sleeping loft, set right beside Beech Creek. Her mother, Margery, married James Jones in the summer of 1884, when the Civil War that had torn at the country the way a crow rips at a deer carcass had been over for twenty years. Margery and James, fair-skinned, red-haired, and blue-eyed, were descended from German and Scotch Irish immigrants. James' grandparents are the same Joneses who left the highlands of Scotland because by religion, they were starving Protestants, and by nature, they were stubborn people whose pride and hard work had sustained them on land that now mostly yielded rocks and heather.

Although large parts of the story are lost, it is clear that the Joneses came to America in 1642, landing in Massachusetts and then working their way south through New York's Herkimer County, through Potter County, Pennsylvania, until they settled in 1740 in Yarnell, part of the Delaware Indians' hunting grounds.

Margery and James built a plank house in a beautiful place— Hawk Holler in the Township of Yarnell on Beech Creek—what the Delaware had called something else a long time ago. Their daughter, Julia, grew up with the Delaware, who taught her about herbs and healing.

Some fraction of all these ancestors exists in Abbey and Ezra, the twins, and also in Eliza. None of them weave or spin as their ancestors did, but they know how to cut and sew; they cannot make or repair instruments, but they can play several, and their voices are instruments, too, when they talk and sing and laugh. Their blood cares how they sound, and they dare not offend it because their ancestors are in their blood, listening. They do cut wood and catch trout, butcher a pig and can green beans. They know how to survive and how to live.

Abbey and Eliza love cemeteries. They like the old cedar trees, the trailing myrtle, the cornerstones with the family's initial cut in. They love the stone angels in the Catholic section, the Stars of David in the Jewish, and the well-chosen granite in the Protestant area. The rose, flint, cream and pale gray stones soothe them.

Abbey took Eliza to the Yarnell Cemetery for picnics from the time she was a little girl. Sometimes it was just the two of them. Other times Dan or Bill or John or Jake would join them. On those days, Eliza learned to predict that one of Abbey's men was meeting them there because of the perfume Abbey wore.

Abbey, Eliza's father's twin, is a Schnable through and through. That is what Trudy, Eliza's mother says, as she shakes her head, her face registering something between amusement and disapproval. When Eliza heard this for about the hundredth time, she asked her, "Mother, what on earth does that mean?"

Eliza, as a curious and willful twelve-year-old, challenged almost everything and everyone—her mother most of all.

It takes Trudy a long time to answer her.

"Well, Eliza, it means she is like your father in good ways and bad. She will give you the shirt off her back, buy you a cup of coffee with her last dime, and ask for nothing in return. She'll also evaporate into thin air when she just can't stand things one more second. And she doesn't know what true blue means when it comes to her heart. Not like your daddy, Eliza, who has a heart of gold. You may want to be like your aunt, but best hope when it comes to your heart, that you're like your daddy instead."

Trudy is baking pies as she speaks, rolling out the dough, wiping her hands on her apron, slicing the peaches and tossing them with flour and cornstarch, butter and brown sugar.

"And," Trudy says even though Eliza thought she was finished, "she loves you as if you were her own. Always has. Always will."

"I like that she loves me, Mom. I like it, too, when she takes me with her to the cemetery for picnics and out with her at night to watch the stars. We use her binoculars to look for Mars, what she calls the bloodstar. But I love it most of all when she tells me stories."

"Yes, well, there's some other things that make her a Schnable—stargazing, horoscopes, divination and stories. You can't eat them, and you can't wear them. Where I come from that makes them not count for much. Anyone who believes you can read the world, or your future, or the past in the stars spends too much time…"

And here she pauses, uncertain about how to finish her thought.

"Well, she spends too much time in cemeteries."

< >

Trudy has the instincts of a wolf. She protects and feeds Eliza and oversees the path she walks. She has pale green, almost yellow eyes that are bright and watchful. She has a dramatic flair for eyeliner, making her eyes appear wolf-like. Abbey often told the story of Romulus and

Remus' rescue by the she-wolf to Eliza, and Eliza especially like the part when their mother, Sylvia, who was condemned to be buried alive, saved her sons by setting them adrift on the Tiber River. Infants in baskets. The mother forced to give them up so they might live. Eliza also felt relieved that Trudy, her mother, didn't have to give her up.

When Eliza was a little girl, the Schnables added the "c" back into the spelling of their name. A sign that Eliza would become a storyteller, a sign that the silence was going to end. Abbey read many Greek and Roman myths to Eliza until she could read them on her own. From the tattered books, she learned a lot about the gods, and she learned a lot about the planets, because Abbey loved science the way Eliza loved stories. Facts made Abbey feel in control and gave her power. She liked them straight up, the way she drank her bourbon. Eliza preferred her facts mixed with fantasy and poetry. She wanted many ways to look at the same things.

The planet, Mars, is named Jupiter and Juno's son and the God of War. Mars, the fourth planet from the sun and the first beyond the Earth's orbit, glows red. Mars, the bloodstar. Look in any encyclopedia and you will find the facts; volcanoes, sand seas, empty riverbeds, and canyons so deep they appear infinite.

Mars is solid, not gaseous, and follows an eccentric orbit. And Mars of all the planets is most similar to Earth, another fact that fed Abbey's and Eliza's imaginations, led them to believe in a different type of life there, perhaps legless and winged—one that flew above the dry, dry ground of Mars, and when it could fly no more, landed in the sand, sliding on its belly, leaving a remnant of blood. And there it rested until it took flight again. Mars, a planet of extreme heat and extreme cold. If water were flown in by rockets to fill the empty riverbeds, the water would freeze or evaporate while it was still being dispensed. That's how extreme the temperatures are.

Abbey announced, "The closest thing to Mars we have here is Nevada. Want to go there, Eliza?"

"Did you already talk to Mom and Dad?" Eliza asked. It is several weeks before Eliza's fifteenth birthday and Abbey has the wanderlust and a plan: she has chosen the trip to fill Eliza with red heat and thirst.

Abbey laughed before she muttered, "Of course!" So off they went to Red Rock Canyon on August 1, Eliza's birthday and the Roman Holy Day for Mars. The air seemed to singe their nose hairs, and the water they carried only temporarily relieved their thirst. When they returned to the hotel, they drank and drank and drank.

Worlds within worlds. That is how most people live. They lie inside themselves the way nesting matryoshka dolls do—a tiny one, inside a small one, inside a bigger one, inside the largest one of all.

A dream within a dream. Like its own world. Like Nevada.

Shortly after their return from Nevada, shortly before Abbey turned forty, the minister was at the table eating fried chicken and mashed potatoes when Abbey decided to talk. "I'll show you my world." Outsiders wouldn't know what she meant by that. But those who know her understand she is talking dirty. She rambles on, talking about the topography of Mars and photographs sent by satellites for her analysis.

The minister stayed and listened to her. "The rocket shoots stars into a woman's world and makes a new universe," Abbey said. The people at the table were accustomed to the mixed metaphors and Abbey's humor, but Minister Wells choked on his soup and excused himself to the bathroom. While he was away from the table, Ezra said, "Really, Abbey, do you have to scare the Reverend?"

"Scare him, hell," Abbey said. "I just got his blood boiling. What do you think he's doing in the bathroom, Ezra, after all this time?"

No one answered, but everyone became more mindful of how long Minister Wells was gone and just how quiet he had become, not one sound coming from the bathroom at the end of the hallway.

Abbey winked at Eliza, and Eliza fled the house to roam the garden while she recovered from her laughter.

< >

"Abbey's dying. You better decide how you are going to tell her," old Doc Schmidt said to Eliza in his weary voice. Eliza now thirty-eight, about the age Abbey was when she took them to Nevada, cannot tell

Abbey anything about her disease that Abbey doesn't already know. Eliza imagines writing Abbey's obituary:

Abigail Ruth Schnable, b. 1929—astronomer, reader, renegade, trained about life and death in the hills and hollows, around Yarnell, in love with the world, the stars, and her family, living and gone, diviner.

If Eliza were asked to write the obituary that is how it would read. Not like the actual one written by Dr. Gillis Peters, Abbey's mentor and colleague, which is kept in her fireproof box and reads:

Abigail Ruth Schnable, b. 1929—astronomer, and lecturer. Trained at Pennsylvania State University, B.S., M.S., Ph.D. Dissertation: Mars, The Bloodstar. President of American Association of University Women, 1967-75.

Abbey went to Penn State when very few women went to college. The few who did go went to study Home Economics or Education, and they went to find a husband and get their MRS Degree. Very few women went to study the planets and the stars.

Ezra Schnable graduated at the same time as his sister in Science Education, and began teaching immediately at the local high school. He joked, "A Bachelor's is good enough for a married man." He felt overshadowed by Abbey sometimes, but mostly he loved her deeply, the way love is at its best, mysterious as one of the canals on Mars.

Abbey refused to teach at the high school. "Showing up every day and telling people how to behave when what I really want to do is study the heavens? I don't think so!" And then, off she'd drive to the library; the only place, she contended, other than cemeteries, where a person can think.

< >

The morphine is not working.

Abbey appears older than she is. She is wearing flannel even though it is summertime. Her hair, what remains of it after the chemo, is white. Her voice is cracked like paint on the east side of a house. Her withered hand grips her sheet. She looks seventy, not fifty-eight.

79

"I gave an old planet a new name, Eliza. That's no secret. My greatest secret is I have a child."

There is a long time with silence, except for the rattle of Abbey's breath.

"Can you forgive me, Eliza?"

And the realization comes to Eliza like cold water on her face in the Nevada desert, like a shooting star landing at her feet, like being set adrift on the Tiber before she is found by the she-wolf.

She is Abbey's child, not Trudy's, and Abbey loves her as if she is her own, because she is. Eliza's heart is pumping very fast and she does not know what to say or what to do, so she goes outside, and in the early morning light, she feels the world and herself being reborn. The stars are fast fading in the morning sky, and high above her, small as a swallow, is an eagle searching for light, and beyond the eagle is the bloodstar, Mars.

IN SILENCE
~ Jane Ormerod

"Yes."

My hands are bleached by the westering sun. I sink and my answer reaches here to there, along your face and through the whitened wall to the garden. As you smile, the room is filled and we breathe a world to one another.

"Yes."

Handfuls of hair web our shoulders. My hand is held. I dream of snow that overwhelms my deepening body. I am rootless and I warm the echoes of you in my arms.

"Yes."

Circles of light hover, slowly spread across the covers, then disappear. I touch glazed skin, your lips slipping pebbles between my spine. Our blowsy limbs swell shadows, we flag our collar bones, raise our necks. We are peacocks, strong and showy. Our blue-bright feathers mesmerize. See our clawing feet, our rapid tails and threaded eyelids broken open. Focus changing, our faces shine.

"Yes."

Leaves wrap the square of sky, veins twisting askew. I clutch at apple scents from the open window whilst the jet stream rumbles. We are oil and water, we slide on sheets of glistening mercury, shake and hold together like blossom.

RENEGADE VOID
~ Thomas Hedlund

The candles always dance. There doesn't have to be any music playing or a breeze slipping through the slit in the windows. They dance. Whether I'm happy or sad, stressed or laughing without abandon, angry or elated. They move in their own rhythm and their own time. They ignore me but how is that any different than everything else?

I have power over them, though. The power of life and death and when it all comes down to it in the end, isn't that what we all long for? That ultimate power over another thing. A little flame may not be much, but it's alive. It breathes, it eats, and it multiplies. If I'm not careful, that is. These three flames are alive because I wanted them to be and they are contained because I wish it so. When it's time for me to go to sleep, their lives will end with a simple pinch of my fingers, like a gnat crawling along the wrong part of my skin. It's as simple as that.

For now, though, they dance, completely unaware of the fate that awaits them. I watch them and wonder what they're thinking. Are they rejoicing in the wonder of life and existence? Are they in the throes of some kind of mating ritual? Or are they simply dancing because they are not me?

I can't stand this place. I can't stand this life. It's dark here, it's always dark in here. And damp. A dampness that seeps in through the fabric clinging stubbornly to my skin. A dampness that chills to the core.

I wish I had something, something more than this brittle paper and graphite stick. My words mean nothing; they're not even tokens of a life worth living. I had no home on the outside, no one who cared for me, no one who missed me when I moved on. Outside I was a vagrant, a wanderer, a bum. I was a nuisance and a menace to society. My words meant nothing out there and in here, they mean little more. I suppose I could relish in the knowledge that I can still do things, if only on a transient scale. My thoughts and memories had always been the only things that were truly mine. I wonder in the flickering light whether I should, or can, put them to paper. Will it make any difference once I'm gone or will the reams of pages be scanned with a scowl and tossed into a sack, carried to the stream I hear babbling by, tossed in and carried to sea a million miles away?

It doesn't really matter what happens to them when I'm gone, I guess. They'll be like my body, a useless shell, a waste of time. No one will take a second look and they might as well toss them in the box with me when they tip the flame to turn me to ash.

This is not remorse you're reading. This is not penance or a search for understanding. I don't give a shit what you think of me. I am what I am. I have taken and I have given, both one and the same, but people have an odd way of conveniently dividing the two. Give and take, quid pro quo, scratch my back and oh, hell. There's no such thing as giving without taking. There's no taking without giving. It's an illusion, trust me. It doesn't take a rocket scientist to figure that out.

You give to the church because you expect heaven in return. You take advice because you've given grief. You volunteer to take away a good feeling. No matter where you turn, the truth always hides in the most obvious places. You choose not to look.

I don't blame you. I wouldn't look either, except for the plain fact that I have no other choice. My mother was a drunk who rarely found time to come home at night. I have no idea who my father is and I wouldn't speak to him if he visited. I raised myself. School? No, I don't think so. I mean, how is the table of elements or knowledge of Ferdinand's assassination going to help me find my next meal? How is that information going to conjure up a place to stay, to hide from the rain? It doesn't. Another example of give and take. The schools want the kids in attendance, but they don't really care about them. They're a bottom line, the numbers that feed the funding. How else can you explain school's complete and utter failure? I'm twice the age of these kids stumbling through graduation and I can write more cohesive sentences than they ever could. Online lingo and the hip gangsta pontifications of the dimwits in Hollywood, that's where these kids learn to talk. Schools pump them through. Give and take, remember?

No, I never had time for school. I had enough to deal with just trying to survive another day. I started working when I was twelve. I lied about my age to get a job pumping gas. I'd sift through the trash at the local supermarket for my meals. I'd cash my paychecks, stuff the bills in my shoe, and wait until I had enough to hop a train and get the hell out of town. I didn't drink. Not then, anyway. My goal was escape. I'm kind of laughing now because I still have the same goal. It's as daunting and hopeless now as it was then. I did it once, though. I think I can do it again.

Circumstances have changed; my surroundings more formidable. A set of steel bars and three solid walls keep me locked up. One guard on each end of the row: never flinch, they never talk to me, and they never fall asleep. I think I'm alone for now, though. They took Dale down the hall a few days ago and that's been it. No new recruits, no lingering prospects. I'm the last one in here. They passed some kind of law on the outside, some kind of tease just to irk me some more, but it doesn't matter. I don't care that they're doing away with it. Once I'm gone, they can feed all the murderers and rapist and molesters they want. I never did understand it much, the debate. So many people crying about how the schools are running out of money, that people are starving in the streets, that the environment's going to hell, and yet they spend millions to keep these men like me alive. No, I don't believe that execution is a deterrent, but I do believe it's a fiscally responsible act. Come on, if you spend a hundred thousand dollars a year to lock up a man for life with no chance of parole and a child starves in the city, what does that make you?

Give and take. You never get something for nothing. I'm not here because I'm a nice guy and that I was in the wrong place at the wrong time. I'm here because of what I did. I killed a man. A cop. I didn't know he was a cop and I doubt that would've changed my action if I did. He got in the way and I didn't hesitate. I told you before, I didn't get any real education, so I wasn't too slick on the getaway. I don't care anymore. It was somewhat of a relief to stop running, to stop hiding and hoping that tomorrow might find better moments for me. They never came. They never would.

I sit alone with these words spilling from me. I've come full circle, I guess. I started out in a kind of cell as my own best friend. I'm still here.

I have to admit though, that the emptiness can draw out like a long winter night. The snows pile up all around, and all I've got to listen to is the hollow howl of the wind coming for me, seeking a way in. It always found me, too, so I'd move on.

I guess I'm a renegade. Always trying to fill the void. To seal the hole.

Some nights, though, the wind is just too cold.

FIRE WATCH
~ Karen K Ford

The day of the hike, Marie had awakened with heartburn, the tiniest ember of it glowing quietly just below the notch of her collarbone. Unusual to wake with it; most often it hit her at the end of the day as she was cooking or folding laundry or just talking to Phillip over dinner. If Phillip had been with her that morning he would have sighed and shaken his head and said, "I told you not to eat those peppers last night." But he wasn't there and Marie knew it had nothing to do with the peppers, had nothing at all to do with what she had eaten.

The night before, as often happened this time of year, she had been awakened from a sound sleep by the pull of an autumn moon a dark sliver shy of full. It had drawn her from her bed to stand at the window with a pounding heart and the undeniable feeling that there was something waiting for her to discover it. Although she knew it was the season when everything was dying, the wild changes of autumn had always felt to her like the world saying yes. Yes to endings, yes to entropy, yes even to death, saying emphatically, *This is happening,* and embracing it completely. It was a time rife with possibility and danger, when she would wake and rise and stare, night after night, sensing some impending change. But that was as far as it ever went; in the mornings she always awakened to the same life, and the significance of her midnight agitation eluded her. This morning her only reminder had been the sensation in her throat—a mentholated blue like the moon, diffuse but insistent. She had lain in bed for a long moment, thinking about calling everything off, but of course she did not have Nick's number at home and so it had been decided for her.

She felt the slow, steady burn now as she walked through the quiet forest, her body's comment on what she was doing out in the woods with a man who was not Phillip, was, in fact, married to somebody else. It could be innocent, she told herself. It could be just a hike to the fire tower to see the view with someone who knows the way.

She cast little sideways glances at Nick as he marched along the trail and compared what she was seeing to what she saw at the office every day. Gone were the button-down shirts and rayon ties and pressed khakis. Here were shorts showing strong, bare legs with tanned, muscular calves, and hiking boots, and a baseball cap to cover the bald spot. Gone were the careful conversations about current events and polite inquiries about weekend plans. Here was discourse on recognizing poison oak or the hiding places most favored by snakes.

It was hot for late October, hot and unseasonably dry. Brush snapped underfoot and dust rose from the trail in spurts, agitated by capricious gusts of wind that seemed to come from nowhere and just as quickly disappear. The usual thunderstorms of August and September hadn't come this year, and though their season was officially over, there was something in the air that made the hairs on Marie's arms stand up and her clothing crackle with static.

"Feels like dry lightning weather," she said.

Nick squinted at the sky. "You think?"

"Feels like something's coming."

"Late for it," Nick said doubtfully.

"Still."

Weather could be a reason not to go on. A lightning strike out here, in the open wilderness, was a reasonable concern. She formed the argument in her mind but swallowed it at the last minute, feeling it stick and then gradually disperse as they walked on, until there was nothing left of protest or reason but the feeling that there was something she'd forgotten to say.

"Are you excited?" Nick asked.

"Excited?"

"About the tower—you've been bugging me for weeks."

Marie's face colored and she ducked her head, wiping at her brow with the tip of a bandana. "Not bugging," she said, almost to herself.

"Really?" she said louder. She remembered when he had first mentioned it, an offhand comment while they were waiting for the elevator. "The view is spectacular," he'd said. "You have got to see it." Marie had recognized the invitation in his tone, even if he had not, and had seized upon the tower as a topic of conversation to prolong those moments when they found themselves together at the coffeepot or the fax machine. One day he said to her slyly, "If I didn't know better, I'd think you were trying to get me alone somewhere." The next day he had proposed this hike. Of course, she'd been forced to accept. How could she refuse after what must have seemed a display of inexhaustible curiosity?

Marie looked ahead to where the trail began its climb into forested hills. Nick had described the route they'd take when he met her at the trailhead early that morning: over a wooded expanse of valley floor, across a creek, less than ankle deep this time of year, to the base of the hills, and up a winding trail to the top of the mountain and the fire watch tower. The authority in his tone and the sureness of his step told Marie that he knew exactly where he was going and she wondered, fleetingly, if he had taken other women on this same journey. Marie felt as though she herself had walked this trail before, but it was only the sensations that were familiar: a quickening that raised gooseflesh on the small of her back, and the occasional quixotic thump in her solar plexus.

"Do you come here often?" she asked and instantly regretted her choice of words.

Nick smiled, acknowledging the joke. At the office he would have countered with something a bit more piquant, and Marie would have upped the ante again, their conversation coiling through a treacherous landscape of meaning, until it had escalated as far as they felt they could safely go. Out here there was no safety; when Nick answered without irony Marie noted that he was as aware of this as she.

"I try to come up with my boys a few times a year," he said. "But usually later, when it's pretty cold. Rugged. You know…man stuff."

In the heat of today it was hard to imagine the cold would ever come, but Marie knew that in less than a month the surrounding hills would be covered in snow. Phillip would take his children skiing then, to Bend or maybe all the way to Mount Hood, while she stayed at home and pretended she didn't exist. She'd never grown used to the days of isolation or his furtive, late night calls, whispered in tones that would not disturb his sleeping children. While he had still been married to Claire, Marie had accepted it as a condition of their circumstances, but now, long after that marriage had reached its inevitable demise, nothing had changed.

"The kids tell her everything," was the only explanation he would offer, until at last her demands had provoked him sufficiently to say: "Look, she hates you! Can you blame her?"

It had stopped Marie's next protestation in her throat. She found, to her surprise, that she could not blame Claire, in fact found her attitude completely justified. After that she had never again complained about being excluded from Phillip's "custody weekends." In truth she found she was bothered more by the implications of his indifference, what it said about what their relationship had become. And while she complied with Phillip's wishes to keep herself a secret from his children, she harbored a secret of her own: that she had begun to look forward, with increasing anticipation, to the times he would go away, leaving her alone. In those moments she knew that the ultimate leaving was not far in the future, and she regarded it from her present position with an interest that was intense but detached, the calm acquiescence of a terminal case.

Marie looked down just in time to see a raised and gnarled tree root bisecting the path, threatening to trip her. She took a stutter step to keep her balance, reaching out reflexively for Nick's shoulder.

"Watch out," he said, steadying her. "Don't go hurting yourself, now."

The trail began to climb, switching back on itself and narrowing, forcing them to walk single file. Scrub oak and Madrone gave way to pines and cedar. The ground was carpeted with dry, brown needles and the air took on the sharp, evergreen scent of the mountains. She walked close behind Nick, watching the shift and bunch of muscles beneath his shirt and waiting for those moments when he would turn to check on her, favoring her with a little smile that she recognized as equal parts delight and apprehension.

At Nick's suggestion they stopped at a switchback to sit on a fallen log and drink from canteens. He wiped his mouth with the back of his hand and beamed at her. "How you holding up?"

Marie smiled back. "Great."

"Not too steep?"

"Nothing I can't handle."

They didn't talk at all then. Marie did not look at Nick and could feel him not looking at her. She concentrated instead on the view: the broad flat expanse of valley floor below, now just a patchwork of rust and brown pulled together by a winding silver thread of water. Except for a short stretch of trail below and another above to the next switchback, there was nothing nearby to look at but trees and more trees but Marie regarded them as though there were something more there to discover. An errant gust, hot and resin-scented, seemed to rise from their feet. It curled around Marie's legs under her shorts and sneaked in through the armholes of her tee shirt before rising to stir the long hair around her shoulders. Nick was digging in his pack. "Hungry?" he asked.

Marie shook her head, becoming aware of the flame burning, more insistently now, in her throat.

"Didn't have breakfast this morning," Nick said, tearing into the wrapper of a granola bar.

"Why not?"

He shrugged. "Left before the boys got up. Saturday mornings we usually make a big breakfast together, you know, the works. We completely trash the kitchen and make enough noise to wake the neighborhood but, man, is it a blast."

Marie heard regret in his tone and imagined him leaving home early that morning, tiptoeing past the boys' room in the predawn dark, fighting the urge to stop and wake them with a suggestion of pancakes. She wondered what he had told his wife about today. She knew it would not have been the truth. There would be some hiking buddy, or a friend in the countryside who needed help clearing brush. Perhaps he had made a show of leaving the house in his khakis and loafers, inventing some office task that couldn't wait the weekend, stopping at a gas station along the way to change into the shorts and hiking boots he'd stashed in the trunk the night before. Nick had never mentioned his wife by name, but Marie knew by way of his careful omissions that she did exist. The source of their unhappiness was unknown; it could be so many things, as Marie had learned, and yet ultimately the reasons wouldn't matter. The outcome would be the same. It was always the same.

"Where's Phillip this weekend?" Nick asked.

"Medical conference."

"Oh. Where?"

"Sun Valley."

"Too early for skiing."

"Golf."

Nick nodded. "Why doesn't he take you with him?" he said after a moment.

"He has, a few times. It's a bore. He's in lectures all day and I'm left hanging out with a bunch of doctors' wives." She stuck out her tongue.

"But you're not a doctor's wife."

"Thank God."

She felt Nick's eyes on her.

"He really should make an honest woman of you."

"That's a very last-century kind of thing to say," Marie said. "Besides, even if I wanted to—which I don't—marriage didn't work out so great for him the first time around."

Marie thought again of Claire, trying to conjure her face from the pictures she'd seen. Her image remained hazy in Marie's mind, no more distinctive than a motif in patterned wallpaper. Before Phillip there had been Mike, with a wife named Angela. And before that, Harrison, whose wife was....Denise? She couldn't quite remember. The men remained vivid in her memory but the wives were indistinct, their images made up entirely of details their husbands had chosen to relate and glossed over with a veneer of pity that Marie herself had supplied, adding to it year by year, like layering varnish on a tabletop, until it clouded over into hardened contempt. Though there had been only three, she often pictured a faceless battalion of wives, standing shoulder to shoulder in rank and file, arms crossed in solidarity, forming a barrier that was at once forbidding and frail: resolute but so easily breached. The image came to her now and for the first time Marie wondered with alarm whether it was not, as she had always believed, an aberrant reflection of her past, but a specter of her future.

She looked at Nick. Beneath her breastbone the tiny flame asserted itself, licking upward. *It will be someone,* she thought, *but it doesn't have to be me.*

Nick held her gaze a second too long.

It wasn't too late to turn back. If they were not yet halfway there she could plead weariness, or remember an early engagement with a friend, and ask to turn around. If they were more than halfway, she would have to go on or risk looking foolish.

"How much farther?" she asked.

"We're very close."

"More than halfway?"

"Way more. Why? In a hurry to get back?"

Marie knew there was no going back—once again the decision had been made for her. She stood and made a show of slapping dust from her clothing. "Of course not," she said brightly. "Just anxious to get to the top."

Nick stood and shrugged himself into his backpack. They smiled at one another and, simultaneously, gestured for the other to go first. There was nervous laughter and then, quite unexpectedly, Nick reached toward her face and for a moment Marie caught her breath. Her eyes widened and her mind formed words of protest that never reached her lips; Nick plucked a dry leaf from her hair and showed it to her.

"Leaf," he said.

"Thanks."

They started up the trail, Nick in the lead again. Marie followed on legs heavy with the aftereffects of adrenalin unspent. Of course he had not been about to kiss her, she thought. He was married, and if he was no longer a man in love with his wife, he was certainly a man in love with his children, and probably far too cautious to place that at risk. This feeling she'd had, that there was something more between them, was most likely nothing more than a restless hope.

The air was cooler high in the pines and the wind more persistent. It made a sighing sound in the treetops, a constant movement high above them that Marie could sense rather than see. The forest seemed more alive now than it ever had from on the valley floor, and as they walked through it Marie began to feel like a part of some larger organism, a single cell propelled in heedless motion towards some specific purpose she didn't comprehend.

"I love the fall," Nick said over his shoulder.

"Me too."

"There's this feeling…" She had started to say, "…of inevitability," thinking it the perfect word to describe the feeling she'd had gazing out her window the night before, but thought better of it. Surely that wasn't something to say aloud.

"Moondoggin' weather," Nick said.

"What's that?"

"This thing Nolan and Nicky and I do. Autumn nights we go up to this spot by the lake and build a bonfire."

"To cook out?"

Nick shook his head. "We just…sit there. Watch the fire. Watch the moon. Don't even talk much." He shrugged. "Moondoggin'."

That's three, she thought. Three times he had mentioned his children. As if to remind her, or himself, of all that was at stake. "That sounds nice," she said.

"Better than nice. It's…" Marie followed in silence as she waited for him to find the words. "I can't describe how it is," he said at last.

Around the next bend Nick pointed out the peaked roof of the fire watchtower above the treetops. One more switchback brought them to the top of the mountain and into a clearing. Foothills fell away in every direction from where they stood. Trees and vegetation had been stripped from the ground around them, forming a wide, jagged patch of red earth. Despite the warmth of the sun, Marie hugged herself against the wind. She felt exposed in the sparseness of vegetation here, a desert spot surrounded on all sides by an undulating sea of trees.

The watchtower stood at the edge of the clearing overlooking the valley, a log cabin on slender stilts two stories high, delicate and precarious as a giraffe. Just outside the shadow it cast, squatting on a bare floor of rock, stood a burly assortment of satellite dishes and weather instruments. Sunlight glinted off naked metal surfaces and gleaming white whirligigs turned in the wind.

"What's all that?" she asked.

"Weather instruments. Satellite dishes: TV, cell phones."

Marie walked to the instruments, drawn to their heft, sensing the watchtower looming at her back. She ran a hand along the white-painted surface of a metal stanchion, feeling it anchor her to the mountaintop, and looked up at a spinning propeller.

"This looks so high-tech next to that tower," she said. "Like it doesn't belong here."

"It doesn't, far as I'm concerned," Nick said. "The fire tower's been here since forever. This junk just spoils the view." He tugged gently at her pack and she turned to see him smiling at her. "Come on," he said softly. "Let's go up."

A steep, narrow wooden staircase led up from ground level, switching back twice before disappearing into the belly of the cabin above. Marie stood at the foot of the stairs looking up through the shadows to the rectangle of light at the top. She put a foot on the first step and it creaked under her weight.

"Are you sure it's all right?" she asked.

"Absolutely," Nick said. "Fire season's over. No one's even up there." He squinted at her. "You're not afraid of heights or anything, are you?"

A bad joke came to her: *I'm not afraid of heights, I'm afraid of depths.* She shook her head.

"Up you go, then."

She started up the stairs, silently berating herself for going first as she felt Nick's eyes on her backside. She wondered if he could see up the legs of her shorts. The thought made her climb faster; she nearly jogged up the last five steps, alighting in the middle of the cabin floor. The cabin itself was little more than a peaked canopy of rough-hewn logs. The walls were just waist-high with open space to the ceiling. Wind blew freely through the open spaces and forced its way through the chinks between logs, carrying with it the scents of pine and desiccation, moaning soft choruses in a roller-coaster rhythm. She stood in the middle of the cabin watching the top of Nick's head as it rose through the floor.

"View's out there," he said and pointed.

Marie walked to the front of the cabin and looked out.

"Oh my God."

Nick joined her, leaning his elbows on the windowsill, and Marie felt the hair of his forearms lightly brushing hers. "Gorgeous," he said.

"It is."

"Told you."

Marie regarded the vast expanse of forest rolling in surging waves towards an unseen sea. On and on it went, farther and wider than she had ever imagined from the sheltered vantage of the valley floor. She wondered how the people who came up here to watch for fires could ever spot one with so much forest to watch. Like trying to watch the ocean—not waves on the shore constantly in motion, changing shape as they broke and reformed, but the flat expanse of open water. Impossible to fix on one point. *How would you spot the beginnings?* Marie wondered. The first wisp of smoke rising from the trees, so tiny, so insignificant in its surroundings. Once it soared high enough to claim your attention it would be too late. But that was your job if you volunteered for this—to watch for the little fires, call out to the world if you saw one starting, send someone to put it out before the destruction began. Before anyone could get hurt.

"How do they do it?" she wondered aloud.

"They just look," Nick said. "You can see everything from up here."

"It's almost too much to take in."

"Most forest fires are started by lightning. They watch for the strike, see if anything catches."

Marie felt him watching her, his gaze warming her left cheek. She looked harder into the distance.

"I can't get a fix on anything," she said. "It's like things keep moving. You know?"

Nick shook his head. "I'm not sure."

"OK, pick a tree, any tree…" She waited. "Got one?"

"Yeah, OK. Got it."

"Now just watch it."

They watched in silence. Marie concentrated, unblinking, blocking out for the moment the presence beside her, seeing only the tree, hearing only the wind through the open canopy of the fire tower. The tree began to swim and blur. Which one had she been watching? Was it that one? Or that one? Soon her gaze, unfocused, widened, and the expanse of trees became an enveloping, wriggling carpet of green. She closed her eyes and swayed.

Nick was there, his arm at her waist.

"Are you OK?"

"I just got dizzy."

He led her away from the railing, her eyes closed and fingers pressed to the inside corners.

"Sit down. Put your head between your knees."

Marie laughed but allowed him to help her sit cross-legged on the dusty wooden floor.

"I'm OK," she said. "Really. I don't need to put my head down." The thought of herself with her head hanging between her knees, Nick kneeling there beside her, shocked her into alertness. Already he was so close she could feel the heat he gave off and smell the scent of his sun-warmed skin.

Nick removed the bandana from around his neck, then unslung his canteen and tipped water into the bandana to moisten it. "Here," he said, offering it to her. "Put this on the back of your neck." She laughed again, embarrassed, and shook her head. But when he did not withdraw the bandana she took it and pressed it to the nape of her neck. "I'm OK," she said. "Really."

"Well, do me a favor and just sit there for a few minutes anyway, okay? Humor me?"

Marie nodded. "Okay."

She wanted to ask for the canteen, a sip of cool water to soothe the burning in her throat, but before she could speak, Nick raised it to his own lips. Something about the gesture, the way his eyes never left hers as he drank, was so intimate that Marie felt as if she should turn away and yet she could not. She watched the mouth of the canteen coming to rest against his mouth, his lips closing around it softly but insistently, his cheeks drawing in as he drank. Spellbound by the sight of his throat contracting with the motion of his swallowing, the droplets of sweat trembling in rough-textured stubble there, and fixed by the burning gaze that held her, she saw, in an instant, everything that would follow.

That by the time he leaned in to kiss her, her own conflicting desires would seem beside the point. There would be nothing more to say. Nothing to see but a ragged blue patch of sky. Nothing to hear but the relentless murmur of wind through the walls and the unmistakable rumble of distant thunder.

PARVENU
~ Robert Joe Stout

Just a small snake, she thought,
A dream she'd soon forget.
But it was real. Wiggled
Out her nostrils over
Breakfast at the Club.
Out her ear at Macy's.
Through the corners of her eyes
While guests met on the stairs.
Too quick for her
To grab or bite, it shimmied
Down each smile she plied,
Curled around the words
She tried to tongue.
And threaded the bright scarves
She tied to veil
Her fear of people's stares
And coughs behind white gloves.

LET THE WIND HAVE IT
~ Randall Brown

I discover her in the basement, uncovered, her lips stained green. When the house ran dry, she drank mouthwash, then cough syrup, finally anti-freeze. I imagine her in the grave, still warm. Instead, they burn her, give her back to me in a vase, handing me the responsibility for the gesture that will define her death for me—the scattering of my mother.

A week after the funeral, my father calls. He wants the ashes. He will do lines of my mother until his synapses can no longer fire. She stopped loving him a year after the marriage—and told him so. He didn't believe her, waited forty years for her to be proven wrong, forty years of asceticism and celibacy and silent waiting. He deserves the ashes, he really does, except my mother did not want to be with him, not in life, surely not in death.

He shows up anyway. I'm sitting by the pool, the vase next to me. It's the end of spring. The pink laurel ends its bloom with drooping leaves that make me think of skin peeling off. I'm high on Xanax, two joints, Celexa, trazodone, some oval pill whose name I can't remember.

"That her?" he says, sitting down, the vase between us.

"Oh Dad. It's endless, the sickness of our family, isn't it?"

"*You* on drugs?"

"Yes, Dad. I'm on drugs."

"Nice. In front—" God, he stops himself. In front of your mother, he almost said. They don't make enough drugs to fix this world.

The silence between us might be endless, might be only momentary. When I notice my father again, he's wiping his eyes. Looking at the sky. Staring into the pool. Blaming himself so I can say it's not his fault.

"Sorry," he says.

"Yes."

He uses silence like a "screw you," only no one else knows it's that, only him. He can't understand why no one gets it, the deep terrible symbolism of his silence, all it says. I'm full of drugs and insight today.

I miss my mother. I do. I miss the briefest moments of clarity when she called with a newfound word—recherché. She'd brim over with excitement. "And it means 'rare'—yes that's what the word means. Rare. And the word itself is rare. Exquisite."

"Pretentious," I'd say.

She'd giggle, really giggle. "It means that, too. Isn't that uncommon?"

My dad clears his throat, reminds me of his existence. "Dad, I know what your silence means," I tell him. "Isn't that something? That I know."

"You're talking gibberish," he says.

He wants to say I gave my mother nothing but unlove, never forgiveness, that I held onto her history as if it were the Holocaust. He would like to get angry, but he's unmade for outrage. He doesn't have the words to say all that. He's deluded, crazy, thinks she's in heaven and happy now.

The nice thing about the drugs is how temporary each moment feels. This won't last, what will the next wave of drug bring, that water sure looks cool.

When I come up from the pool bottom into the air, the vase and my father are gone. They're shuffling up the steps, his legs stiff from the Parkinson's, his tongue stuck out as if to taste what might fall out.

Oh, the stupid thing I do. It's easy overtaking him. I more crash into his back than tackle him. He tumbles forward, his head barely misses the driveway, the vase and ashes leave his hand and, blame the drugs maybe, but the vase and ashes do not find the macadam or the boulders lining the driveway; instead the two continue their upward flight, unheeding gravity and my father's desire to hold on forever.

He sobs. What's become of everything! I only add to the meaninglessness he's found at the end of his own life. I've been terrible and selfish. I know! But who cares anymore—we are free, Dad, free, can't you feel it—but he can only bend like the plastic figures of my childhood.

Oh, so poor and broken. So stuck and twisted.

The world pulses—a day-glo heart. My father has become tangled in my legs, as if we were roots. I know that it's not that he cannot move; he doesn't want to. So I hold him, cradle his head as if he were a newborn with new limbs and a new heart and an entire life in which to fall in love.

CHANNELING
~ Lisa Haviland

through, like water
passes by
without pause
These strung-together
intimacies feel
so insoluble.
Today
a trap drawer
has damned off
the waves bred
by his hands, her
waist, those miles
away.

ADDICTION
~ Lisa Haviland

White-trash junkie
in your cuffed sleeves
and black boots:
Standard Issue.
A bird with clipped wings,
pecking
a
way
with
you.

THIS
~ Daniel Coshnear

She thinks, I spend more time on these roads around home than I do at home. She thinks, *this* is probably not so, but it feels so. "The windshield is my front porch," she says to the spaced-out toddler in the backseat. "This" with an open-handed gesture left to right like reading, "this" loosely indicating the vineyard descending to dusty shoulder and graying black yellow-dashed two-lane, dropping down again to more vineyard, champagne grapes, broad leaves in a late summer pale color wheel "this" above, a wide swath of powder blue, a single power line perpendicular right poorly framing a copse of laurels beyond the edge of the zippering fields, and the riparian tangle below with the darker green leaves and vines of blackberry, "this" where a thin shelf of fog hangs over the buried river, persists against the emerging morning sun. At fifty-eight miles per hour the view soon changes, trees closing in, some relief for the tired eyes, shadows across the road, a slight rise and dip and curve, she reads a toppling woodpile, a dry brown lawn offset by the gangly, almost electric patches of pink ladies lining the gravel drive, now the house coming fully into view, "this" unfinished white aluminum over brown shingle, not rustic but dirty-looking, "this" not her home, someone's home perhaps, but yes, her home, her view, a part of her inner circle when you consider the paths she beats day in day out.

Home is the view through the window above her kitchen sink. And the view into the sink, a leaf of lettuce floating, still water, soap bubbles retreating.

Home is the bright light of the refrigerator in the otherwise dark kitchen, the shelves overstuffed with condiments, culinary ambitions poorly sealed, crusted, and the sound the door makes on its tired hinges, and the smell of a withering cabbage.

Home is her fish-eye reflection at the ATM machine, and the face behind the cash register at Safeway, and her toddler's tongue that won't stand aside for the battery powered toothbrush, and the back of her husband's head and the way his shirt puffs above his belt line, and the blinking circle she remembers as her daughter made her wait for the newest hottest thing on YouTube to finish loading, and the way her daughter stood in the bathroom doorway combing out her bangs, and the way her daughter whined, and the way she laughed with her fists pumping the air like a skier about to spring off a slope, and the jangle of her bracelets, and all the memories of her daughter, all of them, and all the photos she can't bear to look at. It happened nine months ago, gestation in reverse, giving birth to death and relentless questions, fruitless how and why and how. Now she asks where am I going and when will I get there. Home is the sight of her own toes beneath the curve of her belly in the shower.

Home is the front walk she sweeps, what had been one of her daughter's chores, and the tuft of dandelion poking through a crack, the ants, the sound of the neighbor's compressor, nails shooting into fence posts, the metallic taste of her tap water, the rancid taste of her ice cubes, the flies circling their circles above her compost bowl.

"Home," she tells her backseat companion, "is a composite of memories, an approximate feeling," but home these days, well, maybe she's too close to see it, like stray marks on a page, incoherent, non-suggestive, a parallax error.

Home is a reach, conceptually. What is it she's really wanting to describe? Consciousness? Unconsciousness? The phantoms that play upon her empty tablet? "Orbits. Habits."

She comes abruptly to a full stop at the second of two intersections heading west through the town of Guerneville. This is where she'd chosen to live. This is where she'd stopped choosing where to live. This is where she'd say she landed, if she'd been flying, which wasn't really so. Home is the ever-thicker clumps of hair in the drain and the dried skin and the dust on the tops of the baseboards. She'd been drifting. The wind pushed her here like leaves against a wire fence. No, that wasn't so either, but sometimes lately it seems so. She'd gotten pregnant. The choices leading up to that event were real enough, cogitated plenty, but so long ago she can't remember. She'd liked him. She remembers. He smelled like sandalwood. He was funny. His moods were easy to understand. They still are. Yes, even now. He was reliable. He still is. They'd wanted to live closer to the city, but no way could they afford it. They'd both been raised in suburbs—they didn't want that. If they couldn't have urban, they'd choose rural. They'd raise her here. She was only a swelling then, eleven years ago, nearly twelve. These pixellated skies? These landscapes without her?

"Look at this," she says. She tilts her rear view mirror and finds her little boy examining crumbs in his lap. "Look," she says. "Indulge me for once." He looks up. There is a family in the crosswalk. One more block and they will come to the river beach. Water flowing. A place to play. A place to rest. "Do you see?" Dad is pushing a stroller, a towel draped around his neck, a floating toy under his arm. Baby's bare feet lead the way, one pointed and the other swinging. She says, "See the baby?" Several steps behind mom is holding hands with daughter. The gentle slope of the brow, upturn of the nose, resemblances are strong in profile. Mom wears a white top, almost blinding in the sun, tied in a bow in back. Her neck and shoulders shine with lotion. But it's the pink and lime strings of the girl's two-piece dangling, bouncing now as she skips and pulls, pointing in the direction they are walking. "Do you see her?" Her name could be May or June or Joy. "Are you looking? Get *this*. Hold it tight," she says. "Now give it back to me."

FRAGILE, PERISHABLE
~ Donna D. Vitucci

After three days of hard rain the sky broke open blue and Felicity headed out to her garden. There was squishing around her bare feet because she wore rubber flip-flops, and the mud juiced between and across her toes, making the whole enterprise slimy. All around her she could hear sluicing in the earth, the water table restoring, the sun inducing shrinkage. The soil sucked up the good stuff while it could, like one day it would be sucking her. Felicity felt a bit tilted, off-kilter. She took Paxil to level off.

With a baby in your arms you couldn't do *anything*, she reminded herself, and that's why she was glad one of her eggs hadn't yet stuck. She had her garden and plenty of things were blooming, or would be, because of all this rain they were having. The earth was fecund. She loved how that word lolled heavy in her mouth, full of portent, a whole world lifted by her tongue. The garden would occupy her this season, and when autumn blew in she'd return to the nesting idea.

The dream of family that had occupied Felicity and Robert in the haziest of manners when they'd first begun trying to conceive, it folded into nightmare because everything Robert did had to be at full tilt. When plain old fucking didn't produce results, they registered Felicity's basal temperature religiously and played by the book. As was his way, Robert read up on the subject, then choreographed their nights like he'd been awarded the directorial mantle of an Oscar hopeful. She allowed him to order her, to pose her, to poke and lift her.

In her mind, the pregnancies wouldn't stick because the babies, poor lost souls, peeked into their future with her and they bailed quick and early, nobody's fools. She'd miscarried twice, was afraid to try again, but her aunts, standing in for Felicity's own dead mother, said, *Third time's a charm.* Three, mystical number. A holy family of three would emerge from all that agenda-fucking, fucking like following a recipe. Tedium and resentment would flush free from Felicity the same way she'd heard the worst of labor fades.

They'd be another suburban family, Gatlinburg-bound in summers, fresh-faced, hale and hearty, eager for hike, strong in muscle and bone. No worries, be happy. Slip Paxil past the tongue. "You're no one special," Robert said. Then he corrected. "Of course you're special. That's not what I meant, honey. But you're not the only woman struggling. Infertility affects a good ten percent of the population. Of those, forty percent are due to *a female factor* and forty percent are due to *a male factor*. So I'll accept half the blame right off the bat, okay? Let's just try to fix this on our own."

Robert, her stalwart statistician. Count on him to know the latest numbers, x chances in whatever. She was sick of the odds. She wanted a loophole, some cheating scheme that would offer a leg up. No surrogate or in vitro or fertility drugs, not yet. Felicity let herself be shanghaied, instead, by what she'd heard her mother and her aunts whisper bits of in their kitchens back on Gunpowder Creek before they all came north to work in the Delta airport expansion. A mix of prayers, the stars, and the earth's power to grow was her heritage and she was right laying claim to it, just as she'd had to suffer Robert's mockery. "Your hillbilly roots," he called them, dismissing the potential for mythmaking that was in her.

"You're Kentucky same as I am," she said.

"Florence is a city, not quite as primitive as creek living."

He had the idea he'd lifted her from some ignorant hollow, though when they met, Felicity and her mom were renting a unit in the complex behind Showcase Cinemas. If Erlanger was what *city* had to offer, she'd take creek-side any day.

She'd been with Robert three years and then moved back in to that two-bedroom apartment to help her mother whip the disease they found eating at her inside, female parts. From the start, cancer had the upper hand, and though her mother put on a good face for when the world looked in, Felicity watched the woman who'd birthed her and beat her bottom red and bathed her as a little girl in an outside tub summers in their front yard whittled down to bones. With the I-75 traffic outside rattling louder than the air conditioner in the window, her mother begged for a last taste of their creek. Morphine already had her out of her head by then. Felicity brought tap water to the bed and lied about where it came from, but it didn't matter, her mother's lips couldn't manage to kiss around the straw.

Felicity shook her head, if only it was that easy to erase. "So what fertility advances do the great city of Florence and its doctors have to offer?"

Robert wiggled his thick dark eyebrows in what she guessed he thought was an attractive come-on. She did find his eyebrows sexy, and his eyelashes too, the way they framed his blue eyes. He said, "Honey, we haven't yet exhausted our homegrown methods. In fact," and here he depressed the button that lit his digital watch so he could verify the date, "now's prime operating time."

He managed to short-circuit romance without even trying. *Trying*—their operative word. From the back patio she'd lugged the large clay pot filled with myrtle and placed it hearthside earlier in the day. Masquerading as home décor, the scent of the frowsy white blossoms would wind its way through the house and into their bedroom. The magic would find them, and bless her.

In the morning she ran to the garden. Her feet splashed through wet grass, she dropped to her knees, hands curled to catch the globes of tomatoes, then fingers pinch-poised to squash grub worms. She felt the dirt on her skin as a cousin.

By then Robert had departed for the office. Felicity reveled in the room to breathe, to run half crazy around the yard, to divide the early summer air with her slim, not-pregnant body. She wondered, did she really even want a baby? And the aunts seated on the judgment bench inside her head immediately scolded, "Selfish girl!" Aunt Mary, Aunt Alice, Aunt Patty, Aunt Clare were all she had left of her mother. The aunts still sprayed their loose blond locks with setting lotion, lay heads down with pin-curled hair on pillow slips stiff from bluing, the way they'd been taught to bleach the bedclothes as girls growing up.

Felicity waffled on the baby: wanted one, didn't want, and then doubled fierce back to wanting. She sometimes felt tacked like a butterfly in a collection of Robert's, under his examination for any pregnant indicator. A baby would trump his to-do lists, loosen up his iron grip, might even smooth his pointed expectations. By accident and innocently, she knew, he was capable of grounding her, his fingers smudging her, erasing her casual manner and that easy suspension of disbelief that had first captivated him. Now he called it gullibility, he put it down as dreaminess. If she gave in to all his logic, pretty soon she wouldn't even be able to lift and dance across the grass.

Her heart was growing heavy. Or maybe that was her belly. Maybe the last time they did it something took.

"Wouldn't be surprised," Robert said when he called to check on her at lunch and she let comment about this inert feeling slip. "Everything's working in our favor. Your temperature spiked, we slid the pillows under to raise your rump and kept the goods from running out."

Felicity cringed when he said, "the goods," when he said, "rump."

"I kept my hands off myself," and here he chuckled, "so you got my best stuff. Law of averages, we had to hit jackpot sooner or later." He sounded like that odds man in Vegas who predicted numbers for the Super Bowl.

Sperm health and motility, such were the subjects of their intimate discussions. With that pillow under her ass, and the slippery trail on the inside of her thigh when Robert finally pulled out of her, she'd lain there in bed, giving an insulting, silent pep talk to those sperm tilted, hopefully, towards the bowl of her uterus. *Who wants it bad enough, huh? Let's see a little competition among you fellas, for Chrissakes.* Like a coach whipping up his players at halftime, or a sergeant toughening his recruits. How could sacrifice not be involved?

Saints and spells had held equal sway on Gunpowder Creek. They were equally practiced and prayed to. Felicity might appeal to St. Anthony but she felt her ask would be drowned out by pleas from shipwreck victims, the starving, the oppressed and the poor, fishermen, travelers, and yes, even swineherds, not to mention the mindless who misplaced their valuables. She'd been able to recite that silly prayer since she was young. "St. Anthony, St. Anthony, Take a look around.

Something is lost and must be found." It held about as much magic as Dorothy clicking her ruby slippers' heels three times while chanting. "There's no place like home." St. Anthony never helped her find one damned lost thing. The voodoo was all in your head.

That's what Robert said when she started on the Paxil, that it was a placebo, she only had to rein in her mind and take her phobias to task. She could beat them if she tried. She didn't need help outside herself. But that's just it, she wanted to whine, she most certainly, definitely did. Two hands to take in the trembling world were not enough.

With pencil on a brown egg she wrote her initials and four fertility symbols. In a shallow garden grave, she placed the egg and ten vanilla beans by light of the waxing moon, planted them the same as seeds. She mounded dirt over it, as if she'd set in an innocent row of beans, patted the ground three times and recited verse. It was officially summer and the moon, with its horns pointing east, had risen late. Robert wandered out the kitchen door, after the ten o'clock news, she guessed, and stood at the patio edge trying to locate her at the back of their property. So loudly the neighbors could hear, he said, "What possible good can you accomplish in the dark out there?"

Felicity tilted the sprinkler spout above the buried egg and as both water and mud splashed her feet, said, "I'm pouring salt on slugs. I'll be in soon."

He waited for her, and when she reached the edge of the patio he set his broad hands on her shoulders to stop her from going on into the house.

"What?" she said, trying to turn and face him.

He held her in place. His voice behind her, in her hair, said, "Shhhh."

A slow breeze set the trees shivering. That waterfall sound of leaves swept all across the yard, and also something more, an out-of-tune xylophone. Felicity saw the patio light glint off silver hovering in the air by the sliding glass doors. There spoons had been hung with fishing line through drilled holes in their handles so they created wind chimes that would greet her whenever she brushed past on her way to the garden. She could imagine sometimes just sitting outside to listen to those spoons play music—the baby spoon from which every aunt and she and her mother had been fed their first solid foods; the sugar spoon that set in Gran's crystal bowl so neatly that the lid fit snug around the stem and kept the sugar fine and sifted, no clumps. Robert had staggered the four demitasse spoons from Mammoth Cave so the emblematic scenes engraved on the handles swirled and gave Felicity that dizzy on-vacation feeling she loved. Encouraged to see her husband could still pull a rabbit out of his hat, Felicity turned, and now he allowed her to. She kissed him and he kissed her back, and the kiss was no part of a schedule.

She clearly remembered sitting, as a toddler, beside her mother on the front porch with the day dying down around them. The aunts, young again, two of them still in high school, sat staggered on the steps, a-gossiping, their backs up against the railing as they lounged, everybody with a cigarette going to and from their mouths. The dusk air turned grey with their blowing. Felicity was listless and her ear hurt and she'd been leaning her feverish little body into her mother, with her head and her arms and the whole top half of her draped across her mother's knees. Her mother said to the aunts, "Look at my-little-girl-lap-blanket." She sucked on the unfiltered tobacco, then bent and blew the smoky exhale into Felicity's sore ear. Felicity treasured the tickle of it, the soothing of her mother's breath inside those whorly parts of her ear, into her hair, and down the neck of her dress. It was her mother she thought of and yearned for when Robert spoke in her ear, when he breathed on her neck, when he unbuttoned her and tasted down the neck of her summer pajamas. They established a comfortable rhythm, to which she was not at all averse. She and Robert shifted and rolled, tearing part of the top sheet free from the mattress. When they finished, Felicity lay mostly immobile as she was supposed to, except for her foot at the very bottom of the bed. She nudged her toe as best she could within that protected space between top and fitted sheet, without alerting Robert, to locate the sprigs of yarrow, lavender and rosemary ribboned up in a square of cheesecloth. They were still there, close and potent.

Along with the rest of the week's groceries Felicity bought a honeydew melon. At home, she tore a piece from one of the brown paper bags and scribbled, "Give me a baby." Then she added, "…strong enough to survive." She'd already been allotted two that proved too tender, and she didn't want this plea making her out as greedy. She cut a slit in the melon and wedged the folded paper into it, then wrapped the fruit in a yellow bandana. Honeydew juice began soaking through immediately. In the utility drawer sat plenty of white candles for when storms knocked out electricity, and Felicity stood one in a coffee mug and then poured dry pinto beans around it until she was sure it would stay upright. Then she lit it on the kitchen counter next to the melon, thinking on her wishes as she struck the match, loving that sulfur smell. Her mother had called her *my little pyromaniac* when she found her girl Felicity had set fire to a whole book of matches and dropped them flaming in the ash tray, their heat so intense the dish broke in two. It left a burn mark on the kitchen table's oilcloth.

"A baby does nothing but tie you down"—her mother's one bit of advice in the church sacristy where she adjusted Felicity's wedding veil. Caution, and probably well-meant, but the confession and regret, unexpected from her own mother on that day of all days, pinged around inside Felicity's ears. She'd felt erased ten minutes before she had to walk up the aisle. Robert said, later, her skin was as pale as the ivory satin she wore.

She didn't know how long to let the candle burn, so she let it flicker on the counter all morning, next to the wrapped melon while she did laundry. Every once in a while she peeked around the kitchen doorway and checked to make sure nothing caught fire and that the flame still flickered. She guessed a baby would require this same kind of attending, this same kind of vigilance. Maybe this ritual was meant to make you consider that. In five days she should bring the melon to the river with twenty-seven cents. And when she stood at the riverbank, what then?

The leaking honeydew would draw ants. Felicity set it, wrapped in its yellow kerchief like the lopped-off head of some peasant woman, in the plastic bucket she used for household scrubbing. Once

113

the laundry had finished tumbling in the dryer, she blew out the candle and carried the bucket to the vegetable garden. Behind the large watering can it was less likely to be seen and questioned by Robert, though he never made the rounds out there.

Each night Robert rubbed her belly before they turned their faces opposite for sleep. Felicity began thinking of herself as Aladdin's lamp. She carried inside her the power to grant wishes.

After she watched his Jetta disappear from their street, Felicity traipsed in her pajamas to the garden and watered the egg. "Until you are pregnant," the magic had read. Felicity thought she could well be watering all summer long.

Each morning more of the soil seemed to have run off, and by Day Five of the Honeydew she discovered an empty gully in the garden where her "beans" should have been sprouting. During the night, a raccoon must have scooped out her egg for his midnight snack. Suddenly, what she wouldn't give, herself, for a hardboiled egg with plenty of salt. Her belly growled and she put her hand to it, half expecting to see at the end of her arm black skinny fingers and gloved palm like the night thief of her imagination. At the garden's edge, all kinds of gnats, fruit flies, ants, and bees collected in the honeydew's juice. Some had drowned there. She lugged up to the patio, with her very human hands, the bucket of rotting fruit. Robert had said she shouldn't even lift a soup pot of water until they saw how the end of the month turned out.

Upstairs she stripped out of her sweaty pajamas, pulled a sundress over her head, brushed her hair and snapped it into a short ponytail, and slid her feet into her all-purpose flip-flops. Felicity's pulse had turned fluttery. It zinged through her arms and legs, with a skid up her spine that lit her like electricity. Before Paxil, this was how she scattered around, unbalanced, the very balls of her feet giving up on her. The idea of going to the river, whatever she did once she got there, gave her a buzz that rose above the flat, sun-stroked morning. She found she was holding her breath and she sat still behind the steering wheel, gripping her keys, willing herself to inhale and exhale the way she'd learned in yoga class. Her front-seat passenger waited in its bucket.

Bypassing the closer-to-home and more secluded Miami River, Felicity drove the expressway into the heart of the city and all the way down to the Ohio. She parked at the Public Landing, then walked along the Serpentine Wall, stepping down towards the water now and again, swinging the honeydew in its bucket so it didn't bang against her knee. Felicity assumed a vacant stare for the three women who didn't have the thighs for the short shorts they wore as they and their half dozen kids sprawled a picnic over several levels of the Serpentine's steps.

She nodded at the two uniformed police officers astride their stopped bicycles, helmets temporarily unstrapped as they guzzled from their water bottles. She noted the young men of indeterminate age in dreadlocks and do-rags, either head gear too hot for the weather, their dark skins made darker with sweat. She scuttled out of the way of businessmen on early lunch who came up on her quick, the collars of their suit coats hooked on their fingers at their shoulders, their ties flapping. Because they'd surprised her, she glanced over her shoulder, determined not to be caught in someone else's way. She wore a vague smile for the homeless guy twenty paces behind her, who couldn't even see her face but might detect her mood from the spring in her step. The calm and balance in her feet slapping the pavement camouflaged her pinball pulse. To the homeless guy she might as well have been strolling, lackadaisical, along the beach with a sand pail, but it felt like the couple pounds of reeking fruit she carried were driving the metal bucket handle past the skin of her palm.

She was desperate to be seen, and so she had been. Felicity sat on the step nearest the river with the bucket beside her. The Serpentine Wall curved and wound as it followed the natural line of the riverbank and its steps did a shimmery dance of reduction in the hot sunlight, a stone escalator disappearing finally into the Ohio. No one came close, no one bothered her. The barge restaurants docked across the way in Kentucky bobbed slightly in the slow-moving river as she rolled the honeydew from its bucket and down the slope into the dirty water, where it sank.

She mouthed a prayer to any unnamed saint who would listen. "Please let it be, let it be." She'd make the petition no more definite than that. The saint would decide what "it" was, and if Felicity merited an answer. The bright sun made her eyes burn and she closed them to squeeze out some tears. A relief, the water her own body made. At least she could produce something.

When she saw the world again, the homeless man stood near her and said, "Why'd you trash that bowling ball?"

"It was a melon," she said, looking across at the floating restaurants. "And the river's already full of trash. One more piece won't hurt."

He smelled like eucalyptus. He wore Air Jordans that had seen better days on others' feet. His voice was inexplicably tender, like a girl's.

The bum collapsed beside her and Felicity reflexively cuddled her purse in her lap, as if she was protecting a child and already practicing: *Don't talk to strangers.*

There was something about the set of his mouth, pursed as it might be after a taste of vinegar or lemon, two things her mother always spring-cleaned with—Felicity could again smell the sharp aroma, could envision the window panes her mother swiped at with newspaper, so clean that birds flew into them full flight, stunning themselves, sometimes breaking their necks.

The bum might have lost home, hearth, health and even dignity, but elocution rose firmly in his throat. "And you tossed the melon why?"

His eyes seemed kind, even wise. They were blue, Felicity's favorite color, bright like the haint blue she'd begged Robert to paint their front door. She remembered St. Anthony, patron saint of travelers. The bum's shoes appeared to have walked countless miles. She confessed to him about the spell, about the miscarriages, about the Paxil and the galloping in her veins, about the egg stolen from her garden. Then she opened her purse, took out her wallet and gave him a quarter and two pennies. The twenty-seven cents sat in his rough palm, magic complete.

He gave her an almost feral look. "Lady, I'm going to need a lot more than that."

After all, nothing but a panhandler. She could hear Robert scolding her: "You don't even have the sense to be scared."

She looked in her wallet and withdrew a twenty. "That's all I have."

He plucked it from her. "It's a start."

Felicity thought she could hear grains of dirt on his fingers rasp against the bill as he made it totally his. He had given her no wisdom or charms to face the rest of the trembling day, so what had she paid him for?

He rose from his crouch and began walking away from her and she looked off to her right, where she'd parked the car, stood, gathering the energy to walk to it.

The homeless man turned to face her and said loudly, distinctly, "You have to want it so bad you can taste it."

She thought about when Robert called out to her in the dark from the patio for all the neighborhood to hear, but she wasn't embarrassed here on the Serpentine Wall as she'd been in her own backyard. The three women with the white flabby thighs, who knew little about fashion but had managed to help populate the earth with their own flesh and blood, they turned their heads back and forth between Felicity and the homeless man as their chattering increased. Their gossip flapped like crows' wings.

He came back to stand before her and bowed ever so politely, sweeping his ball cap from his head, facing the steps, "Can I take you to lunch, madam?"

Without the cap to restrain it, the bum's hair fell to his shoulders, and Felicity thought she saw his features rearrange into her mother's. Absurd, but he gave her a look reminiscent of one she'd caught so many times, a *Watch your step, missy,* look. Two years ago now, she and the aunts had taken her mother home and buried her in the family plot that sloped down to the creek. Of course this bum was not Felicity's mother, but she was a woman.

Felicity begged off on the lunch offer. The twenty was the bum's now. The money, once given, could not cross back to her in any way but that bad luck would be at its heels.

While she drove home with the air conditioning blasting her and the empty bucket, Felicity mulled what the bum had said. She had a way of ruining things with her longing. This she knew about herself, but was helpless to stop it. Two traffic lights ahead loomed the Golden Arches. She felt capable right then of gobbling down a double cheeseburger without even chewing. Her insides were full of teeth. They'd do all the gnashing required. Though earlier she had eaten that hardboiled egg she'd craved, she now wanted something else in her mouth, substantial meat and bread followed by a sweet taste, maybe some orange juice or granola.

But she stopped nowhere for food, pulled at last into her driveway, took up her purse and the bucket's metal handle, so weightless it was almost obscene. The hot white of midday reflected off the concrete, made her eyes ache, gave her good reason to faint, but she bucked up enough to work her stuttering key in the lock of the blue door. The cool air from inside swept across her temples, where it was so very welcome.

She came home to find the familiar smear of blood in her underwear. The heaviness, the jittery feeling of the morning, it all made sense. She didn't know how much longer she could go on doing this.

"You'll do it until you get it right," she could hear her mother say. Words that accompanied any of a dozen lessons from her childhood—how you're to make a well in a bowl of cornmeal for stirring in the eggs and buttermilk, and breading and frying tomatoes so their slices didn't fall apart in the skillet. One thing for sure, her mother never let her quit an endeavor, even if she made fun of Felicity, even when she said, "You'd never catch me doing that." She recalled, suddenly, another of her mother's caveats from that brief pre-bridal intimacy in the church they'd shared: "Whatever you choose, you choose for the longhaul."

The ringing telephone roused her from the bathroom. The caller ID posted Robert's work number. Past lunchtime and so he maybe worried a little that he hadn't been able to reach her, to tell her, as he usually did, to take it easy, to nap if necessary, to do whatever her body asked of her. She couldn't summon words in her mouth to speak so she just stared at the phone, let him think she was unavailable.

Felicity lay on her back atop the summer bedspread, kicked off her flip-flops, and saw the city grime mixed with sweat that marked the tops of her feet. She wouldn't stop trying. There were plenty of other spells and prayers, and even medical science if they chose to delve there. In a day or two her energy would start rebounding. But she could also hear her mother: *A baby's no solution, just another arm on the octopus.* It was becoming habit, her mother's ghost weighing in with her two cents' worth.

Might take many times before you get it right. Then the stridency in her mother's voice weakened. *There's no shame in practice.*

Felicity was prepared to open her legs to her husband, a stall tactic, as a baby and even sex was, but they'd need to find new ways to be good to one another or they'd find themselves with less hope than the woman begging strangers at the river for lunch money. Felicity went down to the kitchen and took from the pantry the canister of rock candy Robert bought her on their last trip to the Smokies. Commercialism might have transformed those streets into tacky shops for tourists, but they still sold some good homemade sweets. Felicity wrapped a big piece in a towel and cracked it with a hammer a couple times, put the candy in a glass as if it was ice. Then she poured gin just to cover. When Felicity was horrified by the pain and blood of her first period, her mother introduced her to this "sweet shine" for cramps. They would soon be coming on strong, she knew, and she hoped to head them off. Robert said such foolishness just gave a hillbilly one more reason to drink. Here's mud in your eye, she thought, toasting the sliding glass doors, her backyard garden, and those musical spoons. She sipped and swallowed big.

PARADE UPON THE RESTING BOY
~ Jonathan Greenhause

The boy's dry palm is poised, placed perfectly
beneath eternity, his form expecting pieces of the sky
to crack, then tumble, with a feverish groan
and carry darkened cumulous cast.
His eyes pierce heaven's carbon shell
through blinking sentinels of stars
unfettered by the clouds' ripe condensation.

His emerald eyes are fixed upon the celestial stage:
A waiting woodwork's made a visible parade
of sawdust, dirt and darkness laid
where the boy's bare feet sink, seep, and press
into the breast of pebbles, grass, tough clay and soil.
His skin is seized, divided, sheathed
by laboring insects in their toil:
Ants' colonies entranced by ten pale toes;
Snails' slime securing humid trails past porous clothes.
His legs shine phosphorescent in this festival
of fireflies tied to his thinning thighs;
Their silent symphony of flashing lights
draws candent circles in the sable night.
The boy's dried lips are neatly lined
with dappled ladybugs' unfolded wings
and ghostly moths that measure absences of flight...

Now all of them are joined within a stillness of the boy
who holds his palms upright, awaits a shift
or sudden downturn of the dusky sky.
A breath is building towards a breeze;
A chill wind's lips embrace earth's figures in decay,
adorned in cloths and quilts comprised
of a myriad of living things all poised

to swim within this boy's stalled blood
and flesh's loosened skin.

RED-HEADED WOMEN
~ Robert Wexelblatt

She burst through the door of the diner, shouldering aside the waitress whose tray fluttered three times then clattered on to the linoleum. He was conscious of a trench coat, a pale face, hands. Marching past the men swiveling around at the counter she halted next to his booth. Glaring through terrible tears, the woman seemed on the point of accusing him; she even raised a finger and pointed at his nose. The silence in the diner grew more ponderous; not a fork scraped a plate. Everybody waited for the coming denunciation, for the sudden drama to reach an entertaining climax. But there was no such thing. Instead, the woman sobbed and staggered against the side of his booth. She was almost hovering over him now, her face no more than a foot from his; had he wanted to he could have breathed her breath. He had no memory of this face, could not recall her red hair. Her tan coat fell open and he noticed how badly it needed cleaning; he saw that she was wearing a denim jumper, a light blue blouse. No, this woman looked only as familiar as any stranger in whom one might recognize many others but no one in particular. Like anyone in such a fix, he tried to read her expression, to gauge his danger. The woman's eyebrows formed two sideways s's and her mouth was drawn down, giving her an air of being both crushed and ferocious. If she had a weapon she looked as if she would use it.

His mind was racing now. She might grab his knife and plunge it in his chest. He put his hand over it. She was strong, he could see that. There had been a sort of desperate force even in that pointing finger. Suddenly, the woman pounced and, reflexively, he threw his hands up to protect his face. She grabbed not his knife but his ears and swung his head toward hers, easily pushed away his hands, and kissed him full on the mouth. His hands flailed helplessly. She pulled away and, with a cry of triumph or distress, fled through the diner and out the door.

Everybody stared at him and, so it seemed to him, with the same accusing look as the woman's. Had he been found out, then?

But if so, what was found out? The woman's kiss stuck to his lips. He rubbed it away with a paper napkin and turned his eyes down to his bowl of vegetable soup. Reluctantly, as if they had been cheated, people resumed their conversations. They were all talking about him. How could they not? His skin tingled with embarrassment. He smarted under their lingering suspicion but worse was that he suspected himself.

Harnett's was not one of those offices that resemble living rooms, commodious and well-appointed, nor was it an exiguous cubicle with unconvincing walls and no legroom. Harnett's office was something in between haven and oubliette, a simple work space he had personalized with a colorful modern print and the old-fashioned leather desk set his mother had given him after his father died.

Little was wanted from him that afternoon, only that he do the worst of his weekly paperwork, the thing that no one else could bear. On Fridays he was left alone. Nobody telephoned. No e-mail awaited him, no faxes. People passed by outside. He imagined that they slowed down, as if expecting to overhear something scandalous through his closed door. Would the story of what happened with the red-headed woman in the diner have made the rounds so soon? The people in Harnett's company adored gossip; he did not. Once, when he had objected to the spreading of some nasty and obviously untrue rumor, McCarthy, who set himself up as an aesthete and a wit, replied that in his opinion gossip was a "reward for the division of labor." He had laughed fatuously at his own bon mot, to prompt the others. Harnett had felt like a prig. He found working difficult. It would have been better to leave the office, go to the park, walk on the grass. Maybe then he might have been able to think things through. He wanted to be alone with his inchoate thoughts, as if his mind were a treasure chest that only needed sorting out. Instead he dutifully started in on the pile of customer correspondence.

This was work that he put off as long as he could, until Friday afternoons. Almost all the letters were complaints, many crude and misspelled, some stilted, fastidious, crammed with crypto-legal phrases; there were always a few threats. He had to watch for the ones from lawyers. Nasty work. Every once in a while, though, a letter of appreciation would turn up, usually written by a woman for whom the company had resolved some problem. Harnett always answered these personally and warmly. In these cases he would never use a form letter. Instead, he took pleasure in dreaming up phrases with which to express mutual gratification. This was the part of the job he relished and, in fact, what made dealing with customer correspondence tolerable. But such letters were "rare as hen's teeth," which was one his mother's expressions. *"This is to let you morons know that I'm telling all my friends about your miserable service and asking them to tell their friends and so on until you won't be able to do any business at all with anybody."* "I have *written to the Better Business Bureau and the Attorney General's Office. I just hope they give you as bad a time as you've given me."* "You bastards! *It's companies like yours that make the Japs lick their lips. You should all rot in hell."* "My poor old mother, she's eighty-five years old, is beside herself *with worry because you idiots sent her the enclosed bill for $85.95 which is obviously a mistake. If you don't cancel it at once I'm going to come down there and, trust me, you don't want that."* "Enclosed please find my letter *of the 29th of last month, your letter of the 16th of this month, mine of the 24th of this month, and the last letter I had from you, dated the 30th. Notice that I have highlighted each of your misstatements of fact. Enclosed also is a copy of my warranty, with relevant passages also highlighted. Send me a new item immediately or in the future you will be dealing with my well-paid and highly aggressive attorney."*

Many of these people's screeds were addressed to him by name, because his supervisor, a big ex-Marine named Joe MacLaughlin, insisted that all customer correspondence go out over his signature. "Can't I use a pseudonym?" Harnett fruitlessly begged. He found it unnerving to see so much fury directed his way, and yet, compared to what had happened at lunch, the physicality of that red-haired woman and her pointing finger, these words now seemed lightweight and distant, a commotion that would never really touch him. He could deal with disgruntled customers through the formulas and argot of bureaucratic palliation. There was no denying, though, that the letters took a toll. No wonder he wrote with such gratitude to those few who took the time to thank him or the company. He imagined these women to be housewives who didn't work and had time on their hands. He visualized them writing on kitchen tables after sending the kids off to school, still in their nightdresses, sipping a second cup of coffee. He found their decency and boredom touching.

Harnett came on an envelope that had been addressed by hand to the company's president and forwarded to him. Inside was a letter on lined paper.

> *Dear Sir or Madam,*
> *I am writing to express my appreciation of your employee, Richard Harnett. I think you are very lucky to have somebody like Mr. Harnett working for you. Some time ago, when I was having trouble with what I'd bought from you (and, to tell the truth, a few other things in my life) I wrote to your company. Mr. Harnett answered me very politely and promptly. He took care of everything (almost). Anyway, I was so pleased I wrote him a personal letter of thanks. Unfortunately, he didn't reply, which I regret, though really there was no need for him to do so and I suppose you keep him mighty busy. Thanking you for your attention, I am,*
> *Your satisfied customer,*
> *Betty Farincello*

Harnett ransacked his memory but could not recall any Betty Farincello. He got up and went to the filing cabinet where he kept the previous year's correspondence but could locate no letter telling of her woes from any Farincello. The files went from Faber to Fahey to Farley to Feinberg. Might her original letter have been sent more than a year back? She said only "some time ago." And what did she mean by those almost suggestive phrases, *a few other things in my life* and *he took care of everything (almost)*? Almost?

Harnett examined the envelope more carefully to see if it might have been opened. Of course the president's secretary had not opened it, but had merely sent it along to him. This was hardly unusual. Mrs. Rothman, a stickler for protocol, would have judged any letter addressed by hand to fall far below the standard of correspondence deserving her chief's attention. Nearly half of all customer complaints were addressed to the man at the top and Mrs. Rothman had stopped opening them long ago. Did the letter delight him? No, not really. To send it back to the president's office would look self-serving and, anyway, the letter would only be bounced back for him to file with a cross note from Mrs. Rothman clipped to the envelope. But was he pleased by the praise itself? He ought to have been, given the scarcity of it. Perhaps on another day he might have taken some satisfaction in hearing he had done his job well; however, the business at lunch had somehow spoiled this day. The incident made the world seem if not treacherous then at least less intelligible. If a threat could be a kiss, praise might not be praise.

For a moment Harnett entertained the notion that the distraught red-headed woman at the Omega diner might be Mrs. Farincello. But this was absurd, or worse, it was literary. Books ought to be extracted from life, not vice versa. Harnett pulled himself together. What had happened was just some mix-up. He recalled a Latin tag, *quid pro quo*, and this made him feel better, the world substantial again. An implosion of the extraordinary was thus explained away and so ceased to be extraordinary. Of course. He had a common face. How often had he been told by people that he reminded them of somebody else? *Quid pro quo.*

The door opened. No knocking. It was his supervisor. "I heard about what happened to you," Maclaughlin said, "at lunch." A former sergeant, a judo instructor, he never wasted time in coming to the point. Harnett was gratified that his boss was concerned but also it bothered him that he shouldn't be asked for his own account, that MacLaughlin should think this superfluous. Didn't people know that gossip is hardly ever accurate?

"What did you hear?" Harnett asked.

"That some crazy woman burst into the Omega and practically assaulted you and then ran out."

"Assaulted me?"

"She didn't?"

"Well, I suppose she did. I hadn't thought of it exactly as an *assault*. She was crying. Did you hear that?"

"No."

"And that she kissed me?"

This pulled MacLaughlin up. It put things in a new light. "She kissed you? You *know* her then?"

Harnett shrugged nonchalantly, as Fred Astaire would. "Never saw her before."

"And you say she kissed you?"

"What did you hear? What made you say *assault*?"

MacLaughlin shrugged too, but not like Fred Astaire. "It's what I heard."

"Who from?"

"But you said it was an assault."

"I guess so. Of a kind."

"So then she kissed you but you don't know her?"

"Now you've got it."

"Could be serious. A lunatic. A stalker."

"Think so?"

"Hell, who knows? People pack guns these days, all kinds of people." MacLaughlin rubbed his chin then pointed at the pile of customer letters. "You think it might be one of them?" Maybe he was remembering how he had forbidden Harnett to use a pseudonym. Maybe he saw Harnett riddled with bullets and already felt responsible.

"I've no idea. I suppose it's possible." Harnett looked up from the letters and paused. "I was thinking it could have been a *quid pro quo*."

"A what?"

Harnett blushed. The phrase and the idea both sounded ridiculous when he said them out loud. "Mistaken identity," he mumbled.

"Look. You think you need, you know, protection?"

Fred Astaire never forced himself to do so, but Harnett made himself laugh.

The afternoon finally ended. Harnett worked right up to the last minute, answering customer mail.

"Please, please try to get it right this time." "What part of the damned thing doesn't work can't you people understand?" "According to my boyfriend, who is a bailiff in the Superior Court, you are obliged to give me a complete refund, no questions asked." "I've called three times with no results, now I'm writing this so that I can have a complete record, a fat file to show the judge how you people do business. The judge can decide if it's fraud or incompetence. I don't know." He soothed, pacified, mitigated; he palliated, propitiated, euphemized; he explained, empathized, apologized. He attached memos to letters and put them in manila envelopes to send out to the right departments on Monday. He worked like a demon. The laborer should be worthy of his hire.

At 5:30, when he was getting ready to go home, Benson and Thorwaldson showed up.

"Dick," said Benson amiably, touching his shoulder, "Len and I are going out. How about coming along?"

Since it was unprecedented and he disliked being called Dick, this invitation aroused Harnett's suspicions.

"Yeah. Come on, Dick. Make it a threesome," said Thorwaldson encouragingly with his big Minnesota grin. "Then I won't have to listen to Georgie all night."

"We'll grab a little dinner, go to a club. Don't worry, you'll be home before witching hour."

Harnett looked from one to the other. He was tempted, today especially. He wasn't eager to be alone. In fact, he had been thinking lately he was alone too much. But there would probably be office gossip. He wondered if MacLaughlin might have put them up to it. He had seemed so concerned. Anyway, Benson wasn't a bad sort and neither was Thorwaldson. They were just a little crude. Benson had been through a pretty rough divorce and avenged himself by telling nasty jokes about women. Thorwaldson, the taller but more recessive of the pair, was Benson's sidekick, the announcer to the talkshow host. No doubt they had also heard some version of his lunch at the Omega. Maybe they thought he could use some cheering up, some male company.

Despite his misgivings he said okay.

They took a taxi downtown to a good Italian restaurant. The waiter, who had an accent, was almost courtly; the lasagna toothsome and not at all heavy. To Harnett's surprise, the dinner proved better than tolerable. Benson and Thorwaldson asked him only a few questions about himself, questions that seemed more polite than prying, chiefly about his past. They offered him their sympathy for being stuck with the customer correspondence. "When I see that pile go in every week I always think, there but for the grace of God," said George. "I wonder how you stand it," Len agreed. Neither referred even indirectly to the Omega affair. Harnett began to think he might have been wrong; maybe they didn't know about the red-headed woman and the assault or whatever it was.

Benson insisted they split a bottle of Chianti with the meal. Harnett enjoyed the wine; it made him feel a good deal better about things, put matters into perspective. Two glasses, he found, were just about right for making the unpleasant look smaller and the agreeable larger.

Over little cups of espresso George and Len discussed which club to take him to.

"What do you think?" said Len. "The Persian Kitty or The Grand Tetons?"

"Let's see now. I think . . ." George drew out his words as though turning the matter over like a connoisseur examining an old vase. "Hm. I think the Kitty, don't you?"

Len smiled at Harnett. "You'll like it, Dick," he said reassuringly.

Harnett did not really want to go to a club. He had had enough to drink already, but he didn't want to disappoint his colleagues, who had been so nice. They seemed to like his company. He had even laughed with Len over one of George's jokes. Besides, he wasn't eager to go home, not yet. Midnight had been fixed in his mind, "witching hour." It was just 8:30.

"All right, then. The Persian Kitty," he said with what he believed was cheerful dubiousness.

They called for the bill, split it equally and got up to leave.

A couple had just come through the door and was being led to a table. Though they tried to keep their voices low, Harnett could tell they were arguing. He looked after them and was a little unnerved to see that the woman had red hair. He took a step to the side to see her face, but the couple vanished into the rear of the restaurant and Len was pulling his arm.

"Come on, Dick."

As Harnett expected, The Persian Kitty was a strip club. He bought the obligatory overpriced drink and listened to his companions appraise the women over the racket of bad music.

There were two platforms, one over the bar, the other on the left side, a sort of stage with shiny metal poles. These areas were brilliantly lit but the rest of the place was dark. The object seemed to be to look at the women while not being seen to do so.

"That one's barely legal," said Benson.

"Which one?"

"The brunette with the yellow stilettos."

"Barely legal, that's funny. Wouldn't you like . . . "

Harnett said little. He didn't feel like talking, but he did watch. Everything about the place was depressing. It struck him as odd that a club devoted to titillation should somehow be so sexless, or rather that the sexuality was so denatured and public as to appear shrink-wrapped. In his opinion the dancers lacked the allure of a bored housewife writing a letter over a second cup of coffee.

Benson and Thorwaldson were intently watching the runway over the bar, goading each other on with color commentary. Occasionally they would ask his opinion and, to be companionable, he would say something of which he expected to be ashamed later. He even went so far as to tell a joke he had heard in college about a hooker and a taxi driver. After they had ordered a second round of drinks, he excused himself and headed for the men's room.

He had to pass near the little stage on the left. There was a changing of the guard, so to speak. Two women were emerging from the doorway at the rear of the stage, all sparkle, legs, stomachs, hips, while the two who had finished their act waited to go in. One of these women had red hair hanging halfway down her back. Harnett couldn't make out her face, but she was the right height. Her skin looked as smooth and white as moonstone under the spotlights.

As he was rubbernecking, someone tapped him on the shoulder.

"Come here often?" she asked without seeming keenly interested in his reply. Her hair was straight and blond, with short bangs cut bluntly. She was heavily made up. Though her eyes were bright she looked tired. Her perfume made Harnett's head swim. He couldn't say for sure but behind the paint and scent she looked familiar.

He asked if she worked there.

The woman laughed and said, "Not really, but I'll take that as a compliment."

"That redhead?"

She nodded toward the stage. "Oh, you mean Leda?"

"I don't know. The woman who just went off."

"That's Leda."

"Oh."

She fluttered her eyelashes and teased him. "You liked her, huh? Rather talk to her than me, then?"

Harnett was flustered. What had she meant by *not really*? "What do you know about Leda?"

The woman shrugged and looked over his shoulder. "Leda's been unhappy lately. Maybe it's her grades."

"Grades?"

"She's working her way through law school. Half the girls here are in school. Dropped out myself. I was an English major, very well read. Hey, want to buy me a drink?"

"I was just going to the men's room."

"All right," she said with a frown. "So go then."

When he got back to the table the blond woman was sitting with George and Len, their heads close together. They all looked up at him and chuckled.

"So," said George triumphantly, "she's a stripper."

"Leda," added Len, "the law student with the knockers."

"Who?"

"That redhead at the Omega."

"The one who assaulted you."

They all laughed.

"You mean kissed him," said the blonde. "That's the way we heard it in billing."

As if a spotlight had been focused on him, another pointing finger, Harnett felt exposed and furious. He turned on his heel and left the Persian Kitty.

Harnett walked two blocks to the subway. The streets were damp and empty. Rushing through a tunnel underneath the city he began to indulge in self-pity. His life was not working out as he'd envisioned it on that brilliant night in his sophomore year when, alone on the roof of his aunt's apartment house, he had looked at the Milky Way and thought he glimpsed the years stretching out before him as a magnificent stairway with golden, spangled steps of struggle, accomplishment, love, adulation, wealth, children, philanthropy, adventure. It had been that glorious, but effortless, puerile, abstract. He smiled bitterly at the child he had been then yet felt regret and also shame, as if he had disappointed a judge worthy of respect.

He felt unclean and dissipated. What a day.

Harnett opened the door on his dark apartment and, as usual, the first thing he looked at was the red light on his answering machine. It was almost always still, a little beacon of disappointment and loneliness. But tonight it was blinking: four short blinks, four messages.

He did not listen to them at once. He turned on a lamp and walked around the living room as though stalking some prey. The day had left him jazzed, caffeinated. He talked to his mother on Sunday mornings. If she had phoned it would have been an emergency. But this seemed improbable. Her health was impeccable and she loved Florida.

The alcohol had made him thirsty. He went to the refrigerator, poured himself a glass of orange juice, and drank it down greedily. Normally he had orange juice only for breakfast. It felt thick on his tongue and tasted different now, acidic and sour. Finally he pressed the button and the machine rewound its tape. There was a short electronic beep.

A woman's voice, not his mother's, inveigled and invited. "If you're there, please pick up." Then there was a pause as she waited. "All right. I'll try again later." Then a click. Another beep. This time she pleaded. "Pick up. Please, pick *up*!" An even longer wait this time, silent, as if with held breath, then the click. After the third beep the woman whined pathetically, tearfully. "Are you there? Oh, why aren't you *there*? Why don't you pick up? I really, *really* need to talk." This time there was a drawn-out pause with audible sobbing. She meant to give him every chance. Then the click.

In the final message the woman's voice splintered with fury. "Pick up, damn you! You can"t treat me this way. I don't deserve it. Do you hear me?" There was a brief pause weighed down with exhausted breathing. "Pick up, you bastard!" Click.

Harnett sleepless, forcing his eyes shut. Harnett insomniac, still tasting wine. Harnett tossing, trying to read about people in whose fates he could not interest himself. Harnett's mind straying to red-haired women declaiming denunciations and passionate surrenders, grateful homemakers, student-strippers, discontented wives. Harnett dancing on the ceiling like Fred Astaire. Harnett recalling Betty Farincello's handwriting, Leda's ivory back. Harnett attending to the city's deep breathing after a week of toil, commerce, routine, hearing only late taxis and the trucks lumbering into the city with all that was required for another week.

Can anyone know on Monday how Friday will end? Are all our acts blinded by their consequences? Once in a while it might point its finger at you, but did life ever hold out its whole hand?

COMPOSITION IN GREY AND WHITE
~ Alan Catlin

The naked man is seen composing
musical notes with a quill pen,
though the score is mostly complete,
he inscribes new movements, charts
mystical imbalances no one can play.
His sacred space studio, is invaded
by his paramour carrying a single red
rose she lays on the pages where unused
spaces are waiting to be filled.
What the lover wants only he can provide,
offering her body as proof that nothing
will contain them; not the mirror their
bodies are reflected in or the shadows
cast by candles burning near the bases of
their tarnished silver holders.
Their skin glistens, a patina of the flesh
flushed with a love that becomes a fierce
moment of lust compromised by creation.
The imagined score lies forgotten, gradually
coated with a sealing wax and a molting flame;
a lost Adagio for Strings, odd arrangements
that cannot be realigned.

MIDNIGHT SIDEWALKS
~ Stephen Kessler

I like it when the waitresses change clothes.
At the end of the shift they shed their uniforms
and step out looking like civilians newly alive,
springing up the street away from the restaurant
to meet their lovers or a group of girlfriends
with whom they'll sit for a drink in some bar
or café where they can laugh at leisure
while other young men or women serve them before
their turn to escape and move the cycle around—
these endless circles whose rhythmic movements
are mimicked by hips in rotating motion
in black slacks along the city's sidewalks
to the endless gratitude of eyes like mine
with nothing to do but watch what passes
from the cheap seats after a bargain meal
served under an umbrella by a bald waiter
on a street behind the cathedral in Seville.

THE DARK LANGUAGE
~ Carol Graser

There is a land in me of you
where we began our dark language of miracles
We met as trees, part of a surprising ring
whose shadows shaped the grassy circle of sun
The tree frogs in my branches trilled
to the squat gray females in yours
The fat moon sat in our limbs
whispering stories of inversion
Our roots curled over each other
in secret and this is where our hearts met
For decades this was how we grew
Every spring we complimented
the others sprightly green, the same
bursting excitement. You were there each
summer day as we eased into our lush feast
of sun, lounged in leafy abundance
We let it all go together, felt the same
night chill, heard each other's sugar
cracking into color, sparks of hundreds of
small dyings. We stood with each others' losses
and wanted winter, wanted ice to test us
snow to quiet our days. We gave into
the white silence side by side

There is this landscape in me of you
When I open my throat from under that sky
and speak to your morning skin
an ancient breeze presses against us. Years
and voices fall away, walls of detail and worry
We are breathing again this sylvan air
birthing the next unknown season

VISIT TO BOCA RATON IN JANUARY
~ Carol Graser

At eighty, his gated world is ice. He's
skittered around the edges of insane holes his

entire life and now, it seems, he's going to make it
It's blue here and hibernating freckles open
tiny brown eyes. Light infuses the brain
Black vultures circle above retirement

The normalcy of bones picked clean, digestion
We visit cement walls of the dead and throw
stones by way of inscription. Our children

are in evolutionary stages, becoming
adults. I knit them mosaic vests of artistic
validation, remember each one learning to swim

These waters are intentionally rising
and our bodies are full of salt

CONTINUITY
~ Bradley Strahan

Not even stone
But only the wind
And the water that flows
Only the breath
That passes
In and out
Only the liquid
That makes our flesh
Less than stone more

Bone and stone
Detritus of fire
The fury of flesh
The furious earth
Cores of fire
Cores of fire
Fire in the flesh
That shrivels and weeps

Fire in the rocks
That melt and flow
The fire that wakes
And sleeps wakes
And sleeps....

Water that weeps
From stones
Wears the bones
From the old land
Fills the veins
Of the old earth
And the new flesh

Repeatable flesh
That never repeats
That weeps
From the bones is
Weaker/stronger
Briefer/longer
Windblown pages
A story paper boat
In a swift stream
The last is not
The story in stone
Words that have
Forgotten meanings
The last is not
The lying bones
The last remains
In wind and flow
Water and fire
Molten suns
And the sons of man

WHERE WE ARE
~ Phebe Davidson

Wind rises off the mountain for days.
    Nights are purple and lack stars. Trees
        bend nearly double but do not break.
Nothing is silent. Nothing is still. Sleep seems

    not to come while dreams sweep
        the restless dark. Voices rise in the wind
without meaning the wind without thinking the wind
    without a word. Blankets are damp

    and have no warmth. All night we
are cold in this narrow bed. All night we hug
    our untongued sleep, rising at dawn to wind
        coming up and off the mountain like

something we might have heard before like
    something we might have longed for like
        something we might have understood
back when we still could speak.

CORNER OF HIS EYE
~ Nina Sharma

He can see them sometimes out of the corner of his eye. He shifts them right to left, left to right. Everything else is tight, reined, still. When he looks at them out of the corner of his eye the stiffness grates and his mind undoes itself like a piece of Velcro. In the center, Julie, red-and-white polka-dot dress, the whitest pearls, she nods, demure, photographs well that way. On the sides, Bobby and Chris. Each one with hands in their pocket, looking bashful, looking down. Why are they all looking down? He wonders.

They hardly come around anymore. He holds his breath for long intervals and when he lets go they are there. First, though, he must stop up his nose; the rib cage must rise, billow, then constrict, a corset of whalebone, and then release, laces of corset undone. Sometimes they are festive, sometimes they have all come in wearing blue shirts and don't realize it. Sometimes they carry the cold in with them, if they forgot to shut a door. They won't come for days sometimes weeks and in the meantime, he'll sit back and watch the scene unfold. People walk by and swat at flies with butter-gold swatters. He watches a swimmer in Speedo take a perfect dive. Listens to the noise the body makes as it breaks against the water. Life passes by like this, life seems to float, thought seem to puff out of the top of his mind, conversations passing like clouds overhead, like floating text boxes. His mother walks by with a glass of lemonade.

In his bedroom, there are books under his bed. The bed is low and when he used to slide his hand under there, it smelt like cool clay. He remembers this now and then the memory retracts, like the tricky wheel that pulls away without even realizing.

Some days are like fish in a tank, got to tap the glass in order to make them move, but Julie, Bobby, and Chris always arrive in time, their own strange clockwork. They dole out memories, unfurl ribbons of all different colors, red, gold. They repeat stories, poses, like a clothing catalog, but funny. Sometimes one of them hangs their feet in the pool with their head down. Sometimes he realizes this after they have left. Sometimes the disconnect is unbearable.

And when he can't bear to see even them, he bends his head low, in supplication, lets two hands press against it, cups it, bends lower and the content just seems to pour out with the tilt.

the physiology of a glance
~ jacob erin-cilberto

eyes of blue

retreating into you
corneas corner me into moodless days
unprotected from sun's rays
i blink to think
and think to blink
could get lost in your breeze
balanced on soft gaze
i graze in iris fields
as my retina yields

to the succor
of your

eyes of blue.

REFLECTION ON SHADOWS
~ Andrea Cumbo

The silver-blue flicker collides with the amber glow of light bulbs; someone is home. On my dusktime walk through the neighborhood, I peer in and see a woman with long dark hair standing in her living room, a denim shirt draped about her shoulders. On the floor below her, a little boy—maybe he's six or seven—sits doing addition.

Or a dinner party is happening in the dining room behind the street side window on the second story. Men and women in their 30s sit around what I assume to be a table—I can't see it from this angle. As I walk by the first time, everyone is sipping wine and chatting, the food long-devoured. On my return, people are laughing, leaned far back in their chairs, legs and feet stretched long beneath the table. Sometimes, I can't see people in these golden-lit rooms. I can make out built-in bookshelves painted in a color that is probably cream. I catch a glimpse of a kitchen, granite countertops agleam in the pre or post dinner emptiness. Maybe I see a lone dog, shaggy and longing, staring out the bay window, a single light left on for the owner's return.

But it's not what's happening inside that pulls out this voyeuristic impulse in me. I don't care if it's a shirtless, hairy guy watching Monday night football or a lithe ballet dancer practicing pliés as she folds socks; as long as the people are living in that soft warm light of evening, I want to be in there. Somehow, in that light, everywhere seems better than where I am.

< >

His hand is stretched into the dusk in the middle of the painting, a pen clutched between his fingers. St. Jerome, the saint of historians, librarians, students, but not of writers, sits, in Caravaggio's masterpiece of light, across from a skull that so resembles his own bald head that it looks almost as if he rests before a mirror, his hand transgressing the glass boundary. The light in the painting reflects back and forth between the skulls, off the white of their pates, but it doesn't refract and bend to show us, its viewers, what is being written. The saint's head is bent forward in study, so beyond intentness, his thoughts are hidden, too.

"See how the light beams down from the upper right-hand corner, leaving everything beyond it in deep, deep shadow," the teacher at the Villa Borghese tells his class. But the light belies the painting because Jerome only has a candle, and he's Inside, in a cave even.

I stare at the shadows, what's left unilluminated, my eyes losing focus, and wonder what Caravaggio has hidden there. A companion, a napping cat, himself.

< >

Maybe it's just all the gold leafing in Fra Angelico's paintings that wins me over. The glimmering light dances right off the page and into my eyes. In his Annunciation at a small museum in Cortona, the light in those musty, dank rooms sparkles off the words issuing from the mouth of the angel and spinning forth toward Mary. I don't know exactly what the angel says, but given typical angelic greetings, I imagine Fra Angelico had him say, "Fear not . . . ." Somehow the shimmer makes that both more and less possible.

Fear not. Such a simple directive, one that the light in these paintings seeks to undergird. Fear not, there's light in the world despite of all the scary things. Fear not, the dark isn't all encompassing. Fear not, the light shines even under the bushel. Fear not.

< >

The light bifurcates her body, her back and feet in shadows, as she kneels in the pocket of light by the window. Her hair tumbles, waves crescenting in the sun's rays, and her hand reaches forward, so much like the Madonna's in sculptures—porcelain, soft, strong.

In Manuel Alvarez Bravo's photo "Portrait of the Eternal," the young woman is combing her hair, perhaps preparing to hide it away, tuck into a bun, wrap it under a scarf. Gather it behind her into the shadow that obscures all but her profile, long tresses, and a hand reaching forward.

I want to be so beautiful, so serene in my solitariness, as I gaze at the printout of this photo that hangs, curling, above my desk.

< >

Tonight, I sit at my computer, a halogen lamp beaming the most unbeautiful of lights on the desk. My curtains are partially open. I can see headlights from a neighbor's drive as they rake my office, not bright enough to wake the orange cat on my lap but with just enough glare to startle me out of my writing reverie. I try to imagine myself standing outside, sneaking a furtive glance into my own window. Yet, I can't split myself into two—one woman in the light and one in the shadow.

So I look to see if anyone is watching me from the street. I imagine a young woman on her evening stroll gazing up at my office, catching a glimpse of the side of my desk, a peek of the white laptop. My face tinged blue from the computer screen, hair disheveled, jaw clenched in concentration. I know what I must look like—an intent emailer, a woman writing a letter, someone checking her My Space page. I must look busy, content, focused—a solid purpose piercing out from behind my skull.

I stand and walk to the window. I pull back the curtains and look out to wave. Only shadow reflects in the hazy streetlights.

SEVEN IMAGES SUGGESTED BY EMPTY AIR
~ Jay Michaelson

The wide tan car hood of a Buick LeSabre
Like the expanse of the unconquered west.

A dry winter without snow or shine,
the oyster-overcast ice,
as imagined by ancient primeval gods.

The reduction of all breath
to a hair parted this way.

And yet also the expansion out of windows
from cracks in the weather
to expanses of amber waves
to include everything but the everything outside,
and to imagine that.

An old resolving note.

A scrap of mail
delivered across the globe
in rain
precisely to its destination,
indicated in the arrangement of ink
somehow stable on the paper of the envelope.

The open point of air, as in a sigh,
that precedes exhalation.

IN THE COURTYARD
~ David Appelbaum

The mist caught a web
and held fast
            its quarry snared
above the marsh-grass
flexed and militant
until the salt air
suckled dry the blades,
and freed the jailer,
so that death might weave
            again
her lovely trap.

TRANSMISSION OF LIGHT OUTSIDE TRADITION
~ David Appelbaum

A cloud of mirror
           mourning
bowed in a dark ring
that holds the dawn sea
in a green cup
           I imagined
pagodas and stone spires
where people talk
in solitary pairs,
their meager life counseled
by the rift
into which tears must fall.

When a grey osprey darted
at the sun's irradiant eye
the glint gave light
to that fissure, I drifted
there a phantom on unloved streets
a caul child
           to my own heart
and its vagaries.

Then a salt wind came
from beneath the water,
within reach above me
that common line
that divides one
           from no thing.

PUTTING LILLI DOWN
~ Natalie Safir

1.
I'm watching her walk an edge
between survival and release,
an old woman dragging her bones,
an innocent entering a forest.
How wide is the ribbon of her will—
is it taut or slack as netting?
Her eyes are clouded uncertainty.
Cirrus threads trail across winter skies.

2.
Flesh is silently leaving her frame.
Daily there is less of her
hunched on the soft cushion.
The bones pronounce themselves outward.
She is an inverted cage
any loud noise or wind could crack.

3.
I ask if she wants to leave,
there is silence in her eyes.
She turns away as I moisten her lips.
At every turn the decision
I will have to make meets me.

4.
I wish her into a sweet sleep.
Let soft fog protect her from pain.
Gentle one who trusted the world.

5.
When we are both ready
the day will be very long.
Ten years. How do I not
continue to care for her life?

6.
I carry her to the car,
one hand flat across her back
grateful she does not make a sound.
At the vet's office she settles her body
humbly on the steel table
covered in dark green cloth.

7.
She moves down easily into slumber.
My hands feel no difference
when the second injection
stills her heart.

8.
Her drift into death is seamless.
Her open eyes are clear dark glass.

Sweet Lilli.

Her box with the chenille pad is empty.
I leave it just as it is.

it was once called
~ r g Gregory

it comes like a convict
squeezing through bars
and is gone before
the promptest siren
it suddenly turns
in the ear or rides
the eye of a thought
before dissolving
i have it in a faint
taste or shudder
an ache like a spring
high in the mountains
it was once called love
and now a longing
for a song to be heard
that doesn't bear singing

POSSESSED
~ P Alanna Roethle

Incandescent sparks against the liquid,

velvet black

Your silken, heavy smothering rope

Across my chest, bound up in tangles of my overgrown skin

The comfort making it hard to take a sip of the bitten air

You rub my foot gently

Underwater pulling me away from the stars

The steam of water slightly warmer than my skin

Obscures your blurred and reticent mouth

Are you afraid I'll float to the brilliant sky

Taking the melting moon with me?

Unrelenting, you affect me harder.

FACETS
~ P Alanna Roethle

He looked at her from behind burnt glass

Noting a crooked eye, hair too stringy

Tried the mirror, and that was no better

Woke up one morning and found the beauty again—sighed, relieved

Balancing, rigid, holding on to one view, one facet

An act, a futile snatch, needing that to push on

To remember why he loves her.

Searching always for that crooked shiny star

Waves of light from years away

You can't see it unless you look away.

Feeling foolish, but he knows sadly if he can't find it again

All will be lost.

ON A BEACH
(vignette from a dream)
~ Joneve McCormick

Shadowy trees wrap around one another, undulate in twilight. Ferns and succulent leaves emerge and fade. A pre-rhinoceros creature with low hanging skin munches lacy grass and indifferently looks my way. Leaving my body on a large rock, I view my pose from above. Hills breathe, contract and expand. The beast quizzes himself then walks toward my body on the rock, stops, drops his head and vanishes. Long, biomorphic shapes take his place. A young boy forms from them whose body grows transparent toward his toes.

My focus shifts to light flowing into my space from an unseen source—and I am in a new, spell-bound land. An ocean shimmers blue, green, gold; the sky is pale rose. The rock I sit on now is bleached skeleton white. I climb down and draw a circle, section it into north, south, east and west. The north represents strength, and here fades in a fragile shell growing large and solid. There is a test of strength to pass before the Master of Games will let me move on.

I close my eyes, feel a hand on my shoulder and open them. A young man is standing at my side, the same that formed earlier but now he's older. 'Snuck-up-on doesn't bode well,' I say out loud, but like the power I feel from him. Determination lines edge his mouth. His eyes are like blue ice in summer.

'I've come as required by the Quest,' he says. 'My name is Adam—I'm from the West. You are my partner in strength?'

'Strength is power well-used. Take your hand from my shoulder.'

'If you're going to resist, I cannot be your knight.'

'I'm used to the absence of chivalry.' Perversely, I recall the line from Satre's *No Exit*: 'Hell is other people.'

'What test do we have with the shell?' he asks, dropping his hand.

'The Master of Games left instructions inside the tip, and we're to get them out without cracking it," I reply. 'The instructions tell us what to do next. They will disappear if the shell cracks.'

The shell is about three feet high, and four feet from mouth to tip. 'It's too delicate for anything ordinary to have lived in it,' I comment, drawn drowsily into its iridescence.

Salmon, ivory, purple, green and blue lights burst forth from its mouth and with them the distant voices of ancient tribes. Its crust, ridged with points, spirals like a ram's horn.

'Only the beauty of a thing can trap a man. That's why it's important to see it whole,' he says, not looking at me.

The voices become louder, speaking in rhythms and ancient tongues. The shell glitters in the sun. I feel his heightened energy and interest.

'It's up to you to be faithful to our mission,' he says.

Barely awake, I feel the beating of my heart before he vanishes.

ROOM IN THE SKY
~ Jerry Vilhotti

Among the room full of objects hung blinds that were blinking eyes when a breeze or wind blew from outside, as the window did not set firmly within its frame, making the boy of eight run downstairs yelling for help; leaving all the little children with big eyes hiding in different places of light inside shadows of cover and all the invading monsters to crawl in a low light that he had asked his mother to leave on; telling her he was afraid of the dark but never saying he was more afraid of his older brother Leny One N who constantly tried to enter his being with his heavy breathing beating into the eight-year-old boy's ear and out of guilt for this child she had to leave alone often in order to go work to a garment factory that would go to union-less South and then subsequently to other countries who paid their workers starving wages, she would squander a few pennies until surface sleep overtook him and then quietly tiptoe back into the room to turn off the light which created even more monsters for him while hearing her sounds through tightly closed eyes; hoping the footsteps were not his eight-years-older brother's entering the room and so many a night his voice would shout out from painful nightmares to all the menacing clothes hanging from atop doors, becoming shapes of lurking monsters ready to swallow him up. His shout encompassed all the frightened children imprisoned with him.

APRIL NUDE IN SIX
~ Derrick Weston Brown

I.

In pose begin

Lip ring speaking mouth
narrative instruction

Pose

Lean elongated shaven
Clean underarm fingers still
awkward uncomfortable model

Naked not a metaphor
But a state of mind

Pose

Nude thought. Taut
concave sweat stream
finger paint replica thirsty water color

II.

Inverted arch swing
A generous tan
Smooth skin peppered with
pigment pieces

Pose

Sphinx form head erect
Meeting at mons pubis

A dark heeled memory underfoot
Contours of conflicting curves

O faceless lady
Identified by prints

Pose

Diaphragm expands contracts

III.

Serene standing summit
secret potential energy
balled into veined fists…
chi building

Pose

Eyes closed focused
On interior
On expanse
Inner escape
Into interior

Rise fall
The belly
Rise/fall
Rise/fall

Pose

Eyes flutter like

falling petals
pose and hold

Await anointing of skylight
illumination
blessings
of bared shoulders
Remember
Nudenot naked nudenot naked

IV.

She is mathematics
Bare necessity in numbers
Curvature and roundness

Symmetrical circumference
lies in the rise of her hips;
A tanned half moon
A breast

Pose

The fall equinox begins in
the shadow of the small of her back

Night looms beyond
below
connecting chocolate dots

Her body reclines
A hand rests between waist and hip
an impasse

Head at rest held by sister hand.

Pose

V.

Block with the left
follow with the right
bicep bubbling with potential

Pose

Back knee bent
cooking calf muscle cauldron
percolating punishment
but
she is no fighter
steadfast statue
knuckled up skin bone mar
row
eyes averted
She is no fighter
Smiles

Where are her scars?

Stand vigilant statue
Hold tight
Breathe shallow

Pose

VI.

With full color fingers
Painters paste a mystical myriad
Of spring leaf seasons
On postcard pictorials

She is the spring eve
Sloping daughter of dusk
Dismembered by man made margins
Recorded and repeated

Like the mynah bird's song.

A stoic stance; shadows encircle
her lower torso

Pose

THE MISFORTUNE OF SHALLOW SIGHT
~ Ernest Williamson III

she slid through the sackcloth
like a silkworm
gracing the sweet softness
of aching movement
of slender shaved legs
and her hair was blessed
with a kink
golden brown
fresh
clean
like the liking
to a week-old kitten
her hands were
sweet perfumes
penetrating the dermis
with intent on making man smile
without reason
but her eyes were darting and gray
uneasy to my own sights
yet her scent
the vitality of her ways
made me a bit greater than a man with common sight
her lack was no metaphor needed
for this iteration
I give you
in fact
my eyes are now driblets for hawks
carrion for foolish men
who seem to eat
with their eyes
I am blind
and so happy to confess

to all of the noisy permutations
of ogling formalities
proud beings
with tearless eyes

MOMENTS
~ Christopher Hart

31 Minutes of Life

They rested their bodies against the crumbling walls of the interior courtyard, exhaustion pressing their shoulders downwards in the midst of a suspicious and screeching silence. Sarah's two male companions straightened their tired, aching backs, exertion visible through the slowness of their movements. Knuckles red and worn from exposure to the elements, the men simultaneously lit hand-rolled cigarettes.

Death remained a permanent fixture in the soldiers' daily lives. As inconspicuous as an elephant, it could not be missed. It enveloped, diffused through, and floated within the air. It was smelled in the grass, was felt in the cold smoothness of rifle butts, was tasted in the drinking water, was heard in the beating of birds' wings, and was witnessed when a comrade succumbed to its advances. And it was clever. By remaining ever so still, it could convince unsuspecting soldiers that their feelings were illusionary; that it was a behemoth that happened to have perished while standing, bones crumbling into dust. This was its magic: it lulled its victims into complacency, causing them to forget that Death could not be defeated, nor escaped, but was eternal.

Without fail, soldiers crossed the demarcation between reality and Death's realm. But the entry was never immediately perceptible. A temporal fluctuation, a realignment of reality's fabric, was not something that occurred instantaneously. Instead, victims resided for moments in this nether-Realm, transfixed by the beauty of the location, until a mini-tremor reframed their surroundings. Shifting, reality's edges shook and bulged against their constraints, and settled into a new conformation: beauty transformed into ugliness, love into indifference, happiness into pain.

28 Minutes of Life

The smoke curled up lazily, resting in a grey cloud above their heads as the artillery bombardment began. Momentarily absent, then present, the wind alternated between powerful gusts and pitiful whimpers. The sun irradiated the crumbling courtyard walls surrounding the men and woman. Traces of moisture visible on large pieces of reddish green stone that composed the walls of the courtyard indicated the gelid temperature for the particular time of year. The verdant green grass in the courtyard moved in rhythm with the explosion of bombshells, ruining the silence, while in the far corner a grove of pink crabapple trees swayed in the wind.

Sarah dreamt of glorious childhood occurrences, small remembrances cocooned deep in the brain, impossible to forget. Before hunger, before the emotional numbness accompanying war, there was: dark blue water at eye level; surfacing from the depths of Charleston Lake; crawling onto a floating dock; cannon-balling into water; falling into darkness; darkness transitioning into pinkness; sliding through pinkness upon a tarnished piece of sheet metal; emerging onto a mountain with a panoramic view in all directions, trees and stones as far as the eye could see; a man speaking—Sarah, are you glad we've made it to the top of the mountain? Answering—Yes Daddy, thank you for taking me; more speaking—Peanut butter or ham and cheese? Responding murmurs—Ham and cheese; more mumbles—Are you tired? Cold? Anything sore? She answering—No, I feel fine; at home, enveloped by the heat emanating from the arched fireplace, warm bed sheets surrounding her feet; a strongly built young man climbing through her window; the man sliding into her bed; a child's toothless smile gazing from the crook of her arm.

Then the dream tilted imperceptibly, its edges spasmodically convulsing, trumpeting the arrival of an entity wholly unpleasant. Innocent memories suffered the broad brush stroke of disease and terror: hideous caricatures of her most private memories emerged from dark recesses, like unseen spiders escaping from orange rusty drain pipes in the darkness of night. Once-immutable scenes became altered, the fine details of special memories morphing, though they retained a similarity to their precursors, an additional torment.

Her screaming surfaced from the depths of slumber, until she convulsed on the green grass beside her companions and woke herself. Her friends gaped at her, frightened but not quite so—appearing more pitiful than scared—as grayish tinged skin, dirt covered fatigues, and thinness reflected from them. She reciprocated their stare, wordlessly communicating the multitude of emotions rushing through her mind, and the men understood innately, having suffered their own nightmares.

Breaking the silence, Sarah quipped, "I hope this siege ends soon." The men continued to smoke their cigarettes, and Sarah soaked in the lingering effects of her nightmares.

12 Minutes of Life

Their silence was punctured by a bomb-shell landing squarely on top of the grove of pink crabapple trees in the courtyard. Brown, crusted, rippled pieces of bark launched into the air, hurled in arcs from the epicenter of the blast to the corners of the compound. In all directions, mangled apple pieces sprayed outwards with blazing hot pieces of metal; pink leaves materialized in every corner of the compound, slowly drifting from the sky.

Sitting in stunned disbelief—soaked in apple juice and covered with tree remnants—the three soldiers watched as the pink crab apple leaves descended from the sky. A dreamlike quality enveloped the scene—the edges appeared to be blurred and fuzzy like a dream sequence from a cheaply produced movie, but perhaps this smudging was only illusory. From the corner of the courtyard, a giant crater winked at the soldiers, who lay opposite the inverted protrusion, and from the sky the pink leaves tumbled like confetti at a young girl's birthday celebration. "Close call," Sarah said.

The soldiers stood upright; heads held towards the sky, they observed the pink leaves sway left and right with the wind and descend upon their army fatigues. "Have you ever seen anything so beautiful?" one of the men asked.

6 Minutes of Life

His query remained unanswered. Instead, as a sense of wonderment simmered through them, the soldiers linked their hands and walked towards the remnants of the grove of crab apple trees. They studied the charred remains as they arrived where the grove of trees had been, their faces containing a puzzled, inquisitive quality—like a child's face when a new experience presents itself. Black, charred soil surrounded the blast perimeter in a fifteen-meter radius, pieces of wood lay strewn about, and stumps of trees stuck up from the ground at random spots. Pink leaves lay upon the grisly scene, contrasting starkly with the dark earth.

Perhaps sensing that they would soon share the same fate as the trees, the soldiers bowed their heads in prayer. Sarah ran her free hand against the crumbling blocks in the wall, feeling the moistness, the coolness, the grittiness, the ridges of the stone. As the men began to cry, sensing the passing and mourning the loss of life, a gust of wind billowed through the courtyard.

0 Minutes of Life

Entranced with the majestic scene, the soldiers heard not the ominous whistling of the shell that would end their lives. Few final words were uttered, or grand gestures made. Sarah continued to feel the contours of the walls, picking at a piece of green moss. Kneeling, the men picked up handfuls of pink leaves, released them, and watched them flutter to the ground. "There is symmetry in everything, even on this forsaken piece of land," Sarah stated. Her companions weren't quite sure they understood, but they nodded in agreement.

Sarah's final thought was of her husband; one man focused on the trajectories of the fluttering leaves; the other man thought of nothing. Then a searing heat ran through their very cores, and the three soldiers felt and became nothing. The moment which every person hurtles toward reached its final destination for the soldiers.

From a distance the scene appeared a grisly parallel to the shell landing on top of the grove of crab apple trees. Pieces of bone, skin, and body parts sprayed across the entire courtyard; an arm, part of a head, and a foot made arcs into the air and fell to the ground; metal hurled in every direction; instead of pink leaves, tiny pieces of Sarah and the two men appeared to materialize over the courtyard; and the walls of the courtyard were covered with specks of red.

The scene, which moments ago had possessed a hazy, beautiful, dreamlike feeling, had morphed into a nightmare: as though the passage of time between the death of the crabapple trees and the death of the soldiers had never happened; as though there was a seamless connection existing between the events; as though one had been experiencing a pleasant dream, when the dream had suddenly morphed into a night-mare. Such is war. Perhaps the pink leaves were only an illusion and all along had been blood and entrails.

EMPRISON HER SOFT HAND
~ Robert Wexelblatt

> *Or if thy mistress some rich anger shows,*
> *Emprison her soft hand, and let her rave . . .*
> Keats, "Ode On Melancholy"

Fernlicht was sitting in the mall's security office holding nothing but his temper. Though nearly all the adrenaline had seeped back where it came from, it left him shaken. On the other side of an undersized metal desk sat the head of security. He wore navy double-knit trousers and a gray shirt with epaulettes and two pockets. An American flag was sewn on the sleeve, perhaps, Fernlicht thought, in case the captain crash-landed in Ikea or Benetton.

Fernlicht spoke slowly, as if to a dull child.

The enraged driver of the black pickup had coveted Fernlicht's parking space. The local police, called instantly by the two rental cops, had hauled the man away. "Whoa there, Joey. Calm down now," the officer had said. They were on a first-name basis.

Fernlicht hadn't even seen the hulking black truck pull up behind him. The driver got out and started right in. Simple as that. Two vehicles and one space. Joey wanted, apparently, to fight for it. Maim or kill for it. Luckily, Mall Security's white SUV pulled up before blood was spilled.

The real police told the mall patrol to let Fernlicht go. But the security men insisted they had to have a statement even if the police didn't, that they had an obligation. "Records, you understand," one said pompously, "incident report."

So Fernlicht was still seated in the office when another guard, who looked all of sixteen, brought in a woman of about forty. She was well dressed and fed, evidently well cared for too. Fernlicht estimated her hair at roughly eighty dollars, blouse about the same, shoes twice as much.

The teenaged guard stood at attention before his captain holding up two sweaters, one pink, one white, both cashmere. Fernlicht took it for granted that the woman had already denied everything.

"Shoplifting, Captain," declared the boy. "These." He gave the name of the boutique and waited at ease. The Captain nodded once and dismissed him.

The woman, still standing, ignored the captain but turned toward Fernlicht, looking down on him. She probably supposes I'm a plainclothesman, he thought, or a criminal.

"I offered to pay," she said to the captain but still concentrated on Fernlicht.

"You always do—when we *catch* you," the captain observed. "What is it, darling, six times this year?"

Fernlicht rose self-consciously and offered his chair.

"Gallant," she whispered, sat down softly and crossed her legs, which were exceptionally good ones. Then, to the captain, "Will you be bothering the police?"

"They're already here, thanks to this gentleman."

Fernlicht was surprised by the bluff. The police and Joey must be long gone by now.

"Mr. Fernlicht here," the captain said, "was attacked in the parking lot."

Her expression of concern was nearly convincing. "Oh. Were you hurt?"

"Not a scratch to face or ego," said Fernlicht. Impulsively he added, "Excuse me. Will you be needing bail?"

She gave a little giggle. It was musical. "Will I, Captain?" The captain made an unintelligible sound. Turning back to look up at Fernlicht she said with a kind of amazement, "You'd really do that? Bail me out?"

Fernlicht admitted that he would.

"That's interesting. Really."

The captain spoke irritably to Fernlicht, dismissing him as he had the teenager. "We're finished here."

Balancing the laundry basket against his hip, Fernlicht flipped the switch at the top of the basement stairs.

He set the basket down and tried again, pushing the switch slowly this time, getting the feel of its uselessness. Something was indeed broken or cut or split. *These switches can work for years and go just like that,* thought Fernlicht who, to put it mildly, was no electrician. With electricity, as with life itself, there's seldom a warning. It's there and then it isn't.

Though he was an adult in possession of the facts, for Fernlicht electricity seemed perilous in a way that, say, plumbing wasn't. Make a mistake with the plumbing and you get wet; one goof with the juice and who knows? Fernlicht preferred taking electricity for granted to thinking about its mystery. But the switch was kaput. It was a moment of truth. Fernlicht, five years a homeowner, decided to pick up the gauntlet.

He carefully removed the plate and inspected the wires in the half-light at the top of the stairs. It was going to be complicated. There were three outlets, two next to the switch and one underneath. He gave himself a pep talk. Sure thing. All he needed was to find a new apparatus exactly like the old one and attach the wires in the same way. But first he had to find the right circuit breaker and this would be hard since the basement light couldn't be turned on or off. He decided to attach a lamp to one of the outlets. Whatever breaker made the lamp go out would presumably be the right one.

Fernlicht had a quick vision of himself twitching wildly then sliding slowly down the stairs. How long before someone would come to look for him? He made a note that, should he decide to kill himself, he ought to alert the police first.

Fernlicht fetched his desk lamp, plugged it into one of the outlets next to the light switch, then turned it on. It worked. Then he went for his flashlight. Amazingly, it worked too.

The telephone rang when he was halfway down the stairs. He stopped. *Thou shalt always answer a ringing phone.* Like all powerfully conditioned responses, this commandment dated from childhood. His parents had taken a religio-moralistic view of the telephone. On the one hand, the network was made up of everybody who had signed the social contract, a tacit clause of which declared that, whenever society rang, you had to answer. Morality depends on revelation, telling the truth, the whole truth, on demand. Locked in our bags of skin, in our private chambers of imagery, our first duty is to manifest ourselves. When he was growing up, the phone in Fernlicht's home was never permitted to ring more than three times. *Macht schnell.* Even more indelible was his parents' reaction when the phone rang after nine o'clock. This evoked fear and trembling, like Samuel being summoned by a ferocious God, and was doubtless a vestige of conditioning by a still earlier generation for whom telephones were reserved for emergencies. *Someone's dead, someone's dead,* tolled the insistent receiver. Ask not for whom.

Where telecommunications were concerned Fernlicht's parents were a transitional generation. Thus his mother combined the panic of nighttime calls with the nonchalance of morning chatter. Fernlicht had suffered from both.

He could remember sitting on the floor in his parents' bedroom. Morning sun crisscrossed the beige carpet. He picked at his corduroy overalls. His mother was running through her list of confidantes, head cocked, gossiping as she applied her make-up. In the corner of her open closet, behind the rows of shoes, lurked the big blue Kotex box. He felt ignored and resentful. The telephone can be worse than a younger sister.

So it was with mixed feelings that Fernlicht stopped on the stairs and went to the kitchen to pick up the phone.

"Hello, Mr. Fernlicht. My name is Ted Fredericks, from Bulloch and Wiseman, investment counselors. We're offering free consultations and would be glad to go over your portfolio with you."

"No, thank you."

It took a moment for Fernlicht to recollect what he had been doing. The stairs, the switch, the circuit board.

Flashlight in hand, he was turning breakers on and off when the phone rang again and he had to go upstairs. This time it was a woman's voice, soft and enticing. "Hello, Mr. Fernlicht?" she breathed. "This is Diane Tunbridge. From the Couples Club? I'm sure you've heard of us. We're a discreet organization dedicated to serving single people like yourself—"

"Forgive me for interrupting, but how do you know I'm single or, for that matter, what I'm like, Ms. Tunbridge?"

"Well, Mr. Fernlicht—*Alexander*, you see, we—"

"No, thank you very much."

Heading back to the basement Fernlicht realized that he had attained the second stage of hermithood. More than half the phone calls he received were of this sort. Change your long-distance service. Accept our credit-card insurance. Buy our bonds. We're doing a survey. Enrich your alma mater. Save the homeless veterans, harp seals, children. Like everyone else he detested telemarketing but it had never occurred to him to do anything about it.

Ms. Tunbridge was the right straw. In that instant the long cord of telephonic obligation was as broken as his old light switch. He would get an answering machine, an evasion unknown to his parents and one that would have horrified them. Yes, when he went for his new switch he would buy an answering machine, a baffle between him and the world.

And that is how Fernlicht came to be at the mall.

After leaving the security office Fernlicht stopped at Radio Shack and bought an answering machine, then, in the hardware section of Sears, found a match for his defunct light switch. It had been an eventful foray for a September Saturday: a dab of electrical failure, irritating phone calls, a dollop of parking rage, interactions with two species of police, an unsettling if flattering scrutiny and something like inchoate flirting with an attractive shoplifter who had impeccable taste. On the way home Fernlicht thought not about the woman but about the lives of mall security officers. One summer during graduate school he had worked as a watchman for the Burns Detective Agency. The interview had been a laugh. Did he have a police record? No? Excellent. Did he want to be issued a sidearm? No? Okay. The pistol was optional, but the white shirt and black tie were mandatory. It had been nothing like mall security. He had been alone in laboratories, factories, a conservatory of music; he had studied European history between his hourly rounds, and phoned the woman from whom he was now divorced. He felt for that kid who came into the office, imagined him failing to maintain his dignity in a hive of harassed shoppers, to pass ungiggled-at through a herd of high school girls. Fernlicht's heart went out to the poor boy. It couldn't be pleasant to have such bad acne, to have to don an ill-fitting pseudo-police uniform, and, on top of that, having to arrest a spectacularly classy woman for concealing cashmere. And not just any woman, but one who was soignée, voluptuous, older but by no means old. Adolescence was bad enough without all that.

The answering machine lay snug in its Styrofoam cradle. Fernlicht did not care to press his luck with things electrical. Not only had the house not been reduced to cinders or his heart fibrillated into quitting, but the new switch worked better than the old one. It yielded a decorous, almost inaudible click when flipped, more feeling than sound. There was even a little pinpoint of light to show where it was should he be fumbling for it in the dark. This perfect repair had been carried out with only one more telephonic interruption, and that was a wrong number. Fernlicht loved wrong numbers. He couldn't be polite enough to people who had no intention of speaking to him.

The profound complacency of successful home repair was upon him as he set about preparing his dinner at seven o'clock. He felt like a stout and competent homeowner, a bit like Mr. Badger in *The Wind in the Willows*.

The phone rang shortly before eight, while he was clearing up. Had the answering machine been set up Fernlicht could have screened the call, which still felt like an evasion of moral responsibility. He could have ignored it anyway, let it ring; and, had he been doing anything the least worthwhile, he would have. He had done it often enough before. In his opinion, enduring the pain of importunate ringing set the moral scales aright.

"What are you doing home on a Saturday night?"

"Who's this?"

"The lady with the cashmere. And the legs."

"Pardon me . . . how. . .why?"

"*How?* Oh, easy. The security cop mentioned your name, didn't he? As to *why*, there are too many reasons, none good enough." She ended on a little upbeat.

Fernlicht didn't hang up. Not yet.

"Why did you offer to bail me out of jail?"

He hesitated. "Slip of the tongue."

"Fair enough. So, how would you describe yourself?"

"Defrocked professor."

"Professor of?"

"History."

"Why defrocked?"

"Just not given tenure."

"I used to think tenure had something to do with a decade— ten *years?*"

Fernlicht waited.

"You're divorced, aren't you?"

"It shows?"

"Mm. And I'm a kleptomaniac, if you haven't guessed."

"One of the rich ones who always pay?"

"My daddy used to write the checks, now I do. But I'm asking about you. *All* men like talking about themselves, in my experience. But professors talk for a living."

"Not in my case. Not any more."

Up to a point, Plato taught, it is profitable to think of a person as a country. Useful questions can be asked. What are his topography, resources, economic prospects? Who are his allies and enemies? Is he well or badly governed? Where does he fall on the freedom/security axis? What is the condition of his defenses?

Considered as a nation, Fernlicht is neither large nor backward. He is an unassuming country, advanced in the sense of having achieved a relatively high degree of cultural and political development without quite reaching the point of sclerosis. Long ago his aristocrats were humbled and gave up their hereditary pretensions. Long ago his militarists came to their senses. His peasants are few in number and prefer being picturesque to starting insurrections. In him it is the professional or middle class that prevails and constitutes the center of political gravity. His capital is a bourgeois town. He is democratic and law-abiding.

The tidy land of Fernlicht is large enough to boast both a mountain range and a littoral, for it is impossible to think of him as a flat, landlocked plain. Fernlicht's economy is moderately productive with scarcely any indebtedness. The country is not greedy. It dominates no markets. It imports less than it exports. He always prefers to treat with other nations—like the land of thugs in pickups, for instance—in peaceful ways. While not unprincipled, Fernlicht resists the moral chauvinism under which some neighboring states like to drape their envy or self-interest. Though not behindhand in grasping his own interests, he is generally prudent in pursuing them, preferring even to sacrifice an advantage to avoid unpleasant complications. His neutralist tendencies have more than once won him the position of mediator, though just as often he has been dismissed as lukewarm. Believing firmly that self-government is the best constitution, he will not readily conform to the policies of others, even those of the so-called international community. He is wary of the occasional surges of populist sentimentality within his frontiers and is too patriotic to be a nationalist.

What rescues the land of Fernlicht from being a stupendously dull place, a spiritual Switzerland, is an instinct for play and a culture of continuous self-criticism. There are also significant tensions among the populace. For example, his mountain-dwellers are stern and ascetic, given to inward anguish and spiritual aspirations worthy of their snowy crags. Those who occupy the cities of the coast, however, though neither lazy nor gregarious, prefer a more easygoing existence and resent being made to feel that their lives are superficial. There is friction not only between regions and social strata, but within them. For instance, the intelligentsia is divided against itself, some doggedly serving the status quo, others despising it; some experimenting with imported cultural novelties, others jealously preserving everything that could be called Fernlichtian tradition; some hammering out bleak or bright visions of the future, others caring only to establish the meaning of the past; some eager to say *we*, others incapable of saying any sentence that does not begin with I.

Plato's analogy is strained when it comes to history, where the personal seems quite unlike the national. The teaching of history was once Fernlicht's profession, so what was it he taught? He taught that history means inquiry and that this inquiry is never-ending, that no nation can be certain of its own history, or free from the periodic shocks of revisionism. Only dishonest and dangerous states that have substituted myth for history will confidently claim an unambiguous past.

Fernlicht's history falls into three crucial epochs. These would be the sudden death of his father, his aborted academic career, and his failed marriage. What these three momentous episodes have in common is, of course, loss. In the history of any nation there are events which the people take for turning points because they appear to end definitively. But this is a misapprehension. Some do not end at all but resonate through every moment that follows. This is pre-eminently true of losses. As everyone knows, the sour taste of defeat lingers far longer than the sweet tang of victory. Triumph stands with its legs spread wide and walks forgetfully into the golden future, whereas defeat freezes the past into an indissoluble block of granite against which the present, so to speak, hones its knife.

Self-reliance is the land of Fernlicht's national obsession. Having fought for its independence, it stands alone, uncosseted and uncared-for, but self-reliant and free.

But of course Fernlicht didn't say anything remotely like this to the woman on the phone.

"History," she repeated. "It isn't the same thing as *fame*. I can understand people wanting to be famous. I mean you can wear just about anything. Tell me something from history," she begged.

Fernlicht cleared his throat as he used to do at the start of his lectures. "Prince Klemens Wenzel Nepomuk Lothar von Metternich died in 1859 at the age of 86, never once in his long life having lost his head. He might have known Beethoven. Beethoven was almost Metternich's antithesis. Beethoven said, 'Only the pure in heart can make a good soup.' Metternich was the kind of guy who couldn't make any kind of soup at all. He was a natural despot, a plotter and a schemer who loved his secret police, the kind of durable operator who's eventually called a statesman. In 1810 he escorted the teenage Austrian Archduchess Marie Louise to Paris where, thanks to his machinations, she married Napoleon Bonaparte. Poor Josephine was put aside. Metternich did this for reasons of state, which is a phrase of which he was particularly fond. You should know that just a few years before Metternich had done everything he could to tie complicated knots around Napoleon, but the Emperor sliced through them at a stroke at the Battle of Austerlitz."

"Austerlitz? Do you know that was Fred Astaire's real name?"

They were both silent for a moment, stalled.

"So," she began again, "you like this picture of Metternich taking the poor virgin to Napoleon?"

"They made babies together. But no, I don't care for the picture."

"Then what?"

Fernlicht had a cordless telephone. He walked around the house as he talked to the woman. He went from the kitchen to the study to the living room to the stairway. He flicked his new light switch at the top of the basement stairs.

"After Waterloo Metternich pretty much arranged Europe to suit his taste and ideas. Five powers, balanced like a chandelier, laissez-faire economics combined with repressive politics. If you weren't at the top ,you were badly off, and it got worse every year. Yet Metternich's chandelier hardly trembled. Then, in the month of February 1848, rioters in Vienna, including university students, overthrew the Prince's regime and he had to flee to London where he was stuck for three whole years without a bite of genuine Wiener Schnitzel or Sacher

Torte. What I *do* like is the picture of Metternich trying to keep down overcooked roast beef."

She made a little encouraging noise. "I suppose you prefer those rioting students?"

"They had their problems, too."

"As do we all, as do we all. Take me. I'm divorced and rich, yet I steal things. I was rich even before I got divorced, but now I'm richer. It wasn't the kleptomania, by the way, as you might think. I mean, that caused my divorce. No, he knew all about that to start with. He said it was what was *behind* the kleptomania."

"What *is* behind the kleptomania?"

"Look. Aren't you going to take my side? I'm perfectly prepared to take yours."

"My wife just went away. To tell the truth, I think it was a level-headed thing to do."

"Was that *before* or *after* you got defrocked?"

"During." Fernlicht said, still playing with his new light switch. "Tell me," he said, "aren't you ashamed of stealing things?"

"Actually, at the moment I'm feeling quite proud of myself. I made it through the whole summer with only one suicide attempt. How many can say the same?"

Fernlicht, now circling the kitchen table, realized that she must know his address.

"What sort of things do you steal," he asked, "beside sweaters?"

"Oh, small things, gadgets, stuff that *folds*. It's really just shopping, no different from using a credit card."

"Unless you're arrested."

"Point taken. I think you should know that I'm on the boards of at least half a dozen charities. Philanthropy are us. You have to give as well as take. And that's not all. Some people have claimed to *love* me."

He laughed. "Would you be one of them?"

"Oh, you *are* clever."

"Not anymore."

"No? But you knew all that about Metternich and Beethoven and soup. I'm just bubbling over with questions. Take the phrase 'the whole nine yards.' I know what it means, sort of, by why *nine*? Wouldn't *ten* make more sense? And the Pledge of Allegiance, that's always puzzled me. I mean is the country one nation indivisible under God or is it *God* who's indivisible while the nation could split up any old time? But if God's officially not divisible what about the Trinity? Just the other day I was wondering what's so wrong about hermaphroditism? I know you're not a physicist but could you possibly tell whether light's made of waves or particles? You're an historian, so do the times make the man or vice versa?"

Her questions weren't innocent, weren't even really questions. To Fernlicht this interrogative flirtation seemed a way of feeling the sweater to see if it was worth boosting. She was acquisitive but not hungry for knowledge.

"Do you collect men?"

"Pardon me. Collect?"

"Or just telephone them?"

"*Men. Them.* All these plurals are so *male.*"

He still didn't hang up.

"Why *do* you steal things?"

"I told you. I can't help it."

"Kleptomania is to theft as melancholia is to sadness," Fernlicht mused aloud. "Compulsive taking, a need to possess. A psychiatrist might say it's due to ungiving parents."

"One likes to feel the world's goods moving through one's hands like water through a trout's gills. It's not unpleasant."

"I'll bet you've had a lot of shrinks."

"And each one comes up with a novel theory. But originally I wasn't shrunk for kleptomania. I mean that came later."

"When did the kleptomania come?"

"Like most deformations, in adolescence."

"And are there side effects?"

"Getting arrested, that's one; meeting strange men, that's another. By the way, what were you doing at the mall today?"

"Buying a light switch and an answering machine."

"Why an answering machine?"

"Telemarketers."

"Can you imagine calling complete strangers one after another? Can you imagine dealing with all that *rejection?*"

He strode into the living room. "You called me. I might have hung up on you."

"Went right across my mind, zip, like a comet."

"How exactly did you become a kleptomaniac?"

"Good of you to ask. All right. I was twelve and royally screwed up. So I went to Miss Dawes, my favorite teacher, the one who made me love Emily Dickinson. You know? *I'm nobody, who are you? Are you nobody too?* So anyway, I told Miss Dawes everything that was going wrong and asked her what to do."

"What did Miss Dawes suggest?"

"Stealing."

"What?"

"Well, it made a kind of sense really. A lot of us have demons we can't get rid of, Miss Dawes explained and said we have to trick them. She suggested stealing might divert mine. Her point was that, instead of doing a *lot* of bad things, I should concentrate on just *one.*"

"True story?"

"True in a way, not true in a way."

"What *really* happened?"

"Oh, it was such a long time ago. Are you going to use that answering machine?" Her voice rose a little. "'This is my letter to the world.' *Get lost.* See? Even to stop speaking to the world you have to speak to it. As for me, I'd like to have someone in my life. Other people seem to. Now, pay attention, ex-Professor Fernlicht. This is *extremely* important. Do you think we're compatible?"

Fernlicht, back in his study now, sat down at his desk and stared at the brown blotter and weighed her question.

"No. I think we're almost completely incompatible."

"Almost?" Again, the hopeful rise at the end.

"I can't stand Metternich and you're clearly a princess. I

never steal and you do it all the time. I can't join things while you join everything. I'm intimidated by telephones and you dial up total strangers. You sympathize with telemarketers; I hang up on them. All we have in common is disappointing our spouses and ourselves."

"That's about the sorriest speech I ever heard. The saddest."

"Sorry."

"Sad."

"No, *I'm* sorry."

There was a silence. Fernlicht wondered which of them would hang up first.

"So," she resumed briskly, "you'll defeat the telemarketers, pledge nothing to the Sierra Club or the Democratic Party, bar all the intruding strangers. You'll live in the desert like that saint the angels fed. You're Greta Garbo? You *vant* to be alone?"

"I wish I didn't want to be."

"Well said. Every shoplifter respects honesty."

"And I admire a thief who pays for the things she doesn't want."

"Now, Professor, how are we supposed to know what we want until we take it?"

"Maybe the things you take don't want to be taken."

She hummed a bit of an old tune, "Someone To Watch Over Me." "What would you do if you got a message on your answering machine from *me*?"

Fernlicht put his elbow on his desk. "Listen to it, I suppose."

"Yes, but would you call back?"

"I don't know."

Her voice was suddenly harder. "No? You really don't? You're determined to be impossible? Okay, tell me one more thing."

"What?"

"Everybody's trying so damned hard to be happy. Mobs of happiness-seekers all over the damned place. Pursuing like mad. Good Americans all. So, Fernlicht, why aren't *you*? What's the matter with *you*? Emotional constipation? A soul made of frozen water? Indifference turned into an universal principle?"

"I, I couldn't say."

"Couldn't *say*," she was mocking him now. "With you even gallantry is a wall, isn't it? You're just *bristling* with ground-to-air missiles, aren't you? Well, I'm *sick* of your type, Fernlicht, and by that I mean the tepid, the timid, the . . . sociophobic. You remind me of that old joke, the one about how a single woman can get the cockroaches out of her apartment. All she has to do is ask them for a commitment." She didn't stop with the cockroaches. She was off and running.

Fernlicht thought of refuting her denunciation, insisting on his camaraderie with shoppers seething through malls, even with thugs prepared to fight for a parking space; he considered saying he too looked forward to coming home from work to a roast and TV dreams, was not above fantasizing about lottery windfalls or even the lightning-bolt of love; he almost declared that he shouldn't be mistaken for one of those who believe themselves happy in their unhappiness, that it wasn't he who'd given up on the warm embrace of his fellow citizens but vice versa. Yet the spark of self-defense guttered the moment it was struck. He found he had no wish to argue that the Land of Fernlicht was in its way a tidy, hospitable country, an estimable little kingdom not unlike Denmark, where melancholia, if endemic, is nonetheless picturesque, where children aren't beaten or permitted to starve. He thought of telling her that the chief lesson of history is that any past that can't become a present is pointless, mere dead weight, or that the original sin is our belief that it was committed against us. Instead he fell silent, enduring her invective. What could Fernlicht say when the language of his Land is unintelligible to all who don't live there? And as her rancor swelled, as curiosity curdled to resentment and rebuke turned to aggression, as this woman, who couldn't help stealing even what she could afford, began to damn him, he let her go on, attending almost with a kind of compassion to what she said, aware of how well defended his frontiers were, yet wishing he could hold her grasping hands and somehow find the switch that would light the dark country where she lived.

PROOF OF SEX
~ Reine Dugas Bouton

I was born with twelve fingers. They were taken off when I was a baby and now only the slightest bumps exist to tell the story. This detail of my life was irrelevant until I shook hands with someone the other day, and I felt his hand pull away almost imperceptibly. Were my hands sweaty, did I squeeze too hard, not hard enough—then I realized, he thought I had a wart. That's what they look like—a dome-shaped, smooth wartish bump at the end of each hand. Oh, that's where I had a sixth finger, I tell him. He becomes interested in the story.

It's a story I don't like to tell because it eventually leads to the probability that my great-great-great-great-great-great grandfather, somewhere in Sicily, probably screwed his sister or cousin. There was inbreeding at some point, and that's where the genetic mutation—the extra fingers sprouted. I'm a little embarrassed about that part, because then, people know that somewhere in my family tree, freaky sex was going on and we were punished for it with our extraneous digits, better known as polydactyly. I don't like people thinking about incestuous sex in my family tree, even several generations back—it reflects badly on me somehow.

The same thing happened when I was pregnant. As my baby bump began to grow, I felt a prickly unease at the idea that now the whole world knew that I had sex. Actual sex. The baby was proof. Doesn't matter that I had been married for two years, and let's not discuss before that, when I had lots of sex because everyone knows that's what you do when you're young, foolish newlyweds. But nobody really thinks about it much. When the baby comes, though, it's tangible evidence, an announcement to society: *I have had sex.* The whole world knows with certainty that you have had sex at least once... It's worrisome—people knowing something about me that's supposed to be private. Not so private anymore, thanks to the bump.

I'm no prude, but my business is my business. If only there wasn't the goddamn proof. It'll get you every time. And not just a hickey that can be covered with a strategically tied scarf—there's no hiding an enormous pregnant belly under a pashmina. A bulging pregnant belly that shouts to the world, "I'm the product of two people getting it on!" God help you if you've had trouble getting pregnant, which of course would be me, because then people imagine even more sex going on. Baby-making sex—desperate basal-body-temperature, it's-time-honey, maybe-this-time sex.

I'd like sex to remain a mystery—ancient, ancestral, freaky sex, even more so. I'd like to think that people don't imagine each other doing it. Actually, physically doing it. But I'm not naïve. This clearly isn't the case. People can imagine all the bumping and grinding they'd like—just keep me out of the picture. Now I'm divorced and not dating, so I'm safe again. Safe from scrutiny and supposition. I've finally found that privacy I'd relished before. Now, there is evidence of nothing. No bumps, no proof. What I do is for me to know and no one to find out.

THE BEGGAR WOMAN
~ Rina Ferrarelli

She was weird even for that mountain town
still medieval years after the war:
all the crazies and dummies out in the open,
hearing voices and talking back,
chasing dogs and pinwheels, ribbons and pretty girls,
or chasing themselves like stray dogs,
and a sad procession of cripples
came begging at the fairs. But all these were men.
Spun out of the home into the chaos of the street,
a woman her husband had put aside.
I heard she slept in the tunneled passageway
outside the jail, next to the church, the rectory,
lying in her clothes on the cobblestones.
What did she do when ice and snow
covered the ground, when the north wind
bit to the bone? We didn't see her then.
She came around in summer, a large woman
laboring up the street, the stairs, knocking on doors.
When she reached our house, I watched my mother,
still in her twenties then, invite her in,
treat her like a friend, like company, and she
refusing, *No, no, not like this,* filthy,
I thought she meant, the dirt ingrained in the skin
of her wrists, her ankles, stuck between her toes,
a stink I couldn't name coming from her.
No, not like this, she said again, her hands,
palms out, taking in as well, (I see it clearly now),
the taint of her scandalous position.

ATONEMENT
~ Suzanne Roberts

Black Rock City, Nevada

Blue scatters the red horizon,
washes the earth with dust.
Women worship in the sun.
Men sail from the sky. The beat
of drums rolls across the desert.
Sand paints the sky into my eyes.
A girl hangs a photograph of her dead,
falls to her knees. I struggle
with not touching her.
Clouds trace wispy shadows
across a burnished sea. The loss—
an afterimage of the sun
burned onto the retina,
blinding but necessary.

SURREAL LANDSCAPES
~ Suzanne Roberts

After I toured your studio, viewed
the enormous oils—the canvases swirling
with gray domes of granite, yellow spokes
of aspen, the green sway of pine,
and cloud-spangled skies—
I dreamt I crawled past the threads
of canvas and layers of oil,
entered the meridian of your painted
world. The mountains melting
in the liquid terrain of your body.

THE URN
~ Suzanne Roberts

She wanted to know where Grandma went,
was shown the cold ceramic urn and told,
Grandmother is here. Wasn't she sent,
the girl asked, to Heaven? Where is her soul?
She watched the urn move from place to place—
a shelf, the mantelpiece. The parents never finding
the suitable spot. That night, the quiet was replaced
by sounds of jagged glass interrupting
the dawn. Beside the window, the mother found
her daughter sitting in early morning light.
Each leg bent beneath her, each formed
the letter V, a small wren posed for flight.
She looked to her mother, suddenly shy,
fragments of bone catching light from the sky.

LINKED
~ Lisa Harris

Humidity held the air low to the ground by 4 p.m., right about the time the magenta four-o'clocks bloomed. The humidity held the fumes from the paper mill close enough to the ground that rich and poor, white and black, male and female, young and old had burning eyes, itching skin. If Tessie were to reach out, she could grab a handful of humidity—thick as cotton.

Tessie sat in The Bee Hive and watched layers of grayness distort the horizon, and interfere with the scents of gardenia and juniper, wisteria and roses. The smothering scent of flowers and the acrid scent of pulp seeped into The Bee Hive and made the air in Miss Jenny's shop even heavier—too thick to breathe, too sour to swallow. Hair spray and bleach filled the air. Tessie watched the clock waiting for five o'clock to arrive so they could leave, go back to the trailer park and hear what Mr. Earl had to say.

She had been able to help out during the day. In fact, she could not imagine how Miss Jenny ran the shop without her or without someone else doing all the things she had been doing. She loved watching Jenny work: she watched with such interest that she forgot for minutes at a time how screwed up her life was. Miss Jenny greeted everyone with a smile that showed love and compassion. Then she got whoever it was in their seat, fastened on a pink smock if they were a woman and a manly black smock if they were a man. She let people look into the mirror for a minute or two, as if she wanted them to remember who they were, before she asked what they wanted to have done. While she talked with them, she kept her eyes on their eyes in the mirror. She kept a real smile on her face. After she listened, she said, "I think we can do that for you." Then she did it.

At quitting time, Jenny said, "Close up the curtains, honey. We're going home." Tessie closed the curtains while Jenny closed everything else down. "Thank you for all your help today, Tessie. I don't know what I would have done without you, sugar. I want you to close your eyes once we are in the car and just try to rest. Can you do that?"

"Yes, m'am, I can." It was as if Miss Jenny was a mind reader. All Tessie had been wanting to do for the past three hours was shut her eyes. Even with her eyes closed, she couldn't shut out the fact that Ray had been arrested and that Laura Jean was still in Milledgeville. And everybody in the legal system was so busy being pleased with arresting Ray that no one remembered he had a daughter whose mother was in Milledgeville, a mother who had been there, off and on, for three years, a mother who lasted on the outside, as it was called, only briefly; in fact, a mother who hadn't even been able to stay a full day at her trailer in Little Bit the last time they sent her home.

"We home, Tessie, and so is Earl. Let's see what he found out."

Tessie and Jenny hurried into the trailer. Earl sat at the counter drinking a Blue Ribbon. His face was screwed into a pout and his ear lobes were bright red. That always happened when Earl was mad.

"You want me to talk in front of the girl, or no?" Earl began.

Jenny waited for Tessie to answer. "I want to hear the truth, Mr. Earl," Tessie said.

"Well, it ain't good news, Tessie. They gonna keep him for a while—maybe up to five years."

"Damnation and chicken feathers." Jenny slammed her fist on the counter, which knocked over Earl's beer.

"Don't worry," Earl said, "I got me a twelve-pack in the cooler."

So for a while Tessie split her time between her trailer and the Conroy's. Tessie helped out at The Bee Hive, and in exchange, Jenny Conroy took care of any trailer expenses, feeling that that was the least she could do for the daughter of her friend, Laura Jean. Later, when Tessie stayed at Annie and Josie's house, nearer the swamp—the house Tessie had envied, the house she knew could be home—Jenny promised to keep an eye on the trailer until Ray came home.

Tessie accepted the offering, joyful to have adults helping her. Josie cleaned houses for money and raised an all-year garden for vegetables. She caught and skinned catfish, butchered hogs, and sold the best cuts of meat to neighbors. She kept the chitlins for herself and Annie, and Josie always shared her food and her love with Tessie Harnish.

Josie liked living away from other people. She liked her old white frame house with its red tin roof. She didn't want to live among drinkers and yellers, mill workers and bartenders. She wanted as few people around her as possible; she wanted to be near the swamp and the trees, the cottonmouths and the frogs, the lightening bugs and the river. So Josie lived on land that had belonged to her family for as far back as blacks could own land, because no one wanted to own the swamp, and she lived far enough away from the river not to get flooded, but close enough to be able to fish and shrimp, close enough to walk down at night and run her hand in the water, stirring up the phosphorous, and watching the iridescent green shine in the moonlight.

Tessie loved Josie because she was connected to the earth. The times Tessie stood beside Josie, she felt thin and tall. Josie had the strength of a man. She had to cut the three-quarter-inch sleeves on her blouses that were store-bought so that her muscles weren't impeded when she cut wood and double-dug her garden. Her big cheekbones rose out from under her eyes like little shelves. And although she was shorter than Tessie and heavier, she was magnificent in her life. "I swear your mama has a halo over her head, Annie." Josie overheard Tessie say this while Tessie was hoeing the garden and Josie was making a foot-high rock perimeter around the flower beds.

"The only thing holding my halo on, Tessie, are my short little horns hidden under my Afro."

Josie was, after all, Ol' Dolly's daughter. She knew about laughter and loving and the magic of stones. Josie was also the daughter of Fuddah Osaha, the 'Geechee witchdoctor and trader. When Fuddah was without clients and without raccoon furs, he worked on Ray's boat. In fact, he showed Ray where the shrimp ran when everybody else's nets were coming up empty. Fuddah worked long enough to get the money he needed, and then he went back to his hut in the swamp. Now there wasn't going to be any more work for Fuddah on Ray's boat, not since Ray had been sent up.

Over supper one night at the Conroys' Miss Jenny broke the news, "I can't keep paying utilities and all at your trailer anymore, and

God knows Earl and I love you as if you were our own, but he and I talked and we think it is best if you stay over at Annie and Josie's for a spell. We just need a little couple's time, if you know what I mean." She winked at Tessie who was relieved, in a way, to be gone from the Conroys' trailer—not because she didn't love them, too, but it was all a little too close and she had been starting to feel in the way when they were both home with her, and a little uneasy when it was just her and Mr. Earl. After all, she had been staying with them a lot over the past four months while Ray was getting sentenced.

Tessie went to Annie and Josie's house within a week of the conversation with Miss Jenny. She kept herself clean and silent at school. She seldom associated with Annie at the integrated junior high school. She didn't want either of them getting in to trouble with the white kids or the black ones, and she didn't want the department of social services realizing that she was no longer staying with her "aunt" and "uncle." They stayed away from each other to protect themselves. But after they got off the bus together at the end of the day, and the bus had pulled out of sight, the girls shifted their books to their outside arms and linked hands, skipping down the dirt road, back to Josie's.

No doubt Annie had a father, but she didn't know him to see him. And the facts Josie gave her were sparse. "You got his nose, girl, coz you sure don't have mine!" Annie had a long narrow nose that looked nothing like Josie's flat one. "You must be someone else's child to have such straight teeth." "Where'd you go to get them long legs, girl? T'other side of this town?" Josie would laugh and pat Annie on the arm. "I don't care what kind of nose you got, and I'd love you even if you had crooked teeth like mine. Hell! I might even love you more because of them."

Josie had lovers, but no one stayed overnight. She hung a wrought iron sign outside her door that read: "Dogs preferred to men." And if that wasn't enough to keep undesirables away, the fact that she was Ol' Dolly's and Fuddah's child, who kept a big brown hound right inside her front door, kept anyone afraid of magic far away.

When the people from Family and Children's Services called the first time, one black person asked questions, while a white person wrote pages and pages of notes. But when the outcome of their report came back to Josie, Annie, and Tessie in the hands of a Chatham County Sheriff, it was fairly simple. He delivered it and then stayed to read it aloud, sure as he was that all three of the females present were illiterate.

To Josephine Osaha who resides on the east side of Swamps End Road, November 17, 1969

Be it known that this residence is not acceptable for foster care. Code 70358 has been violated in the following ways: unvaccinated hound; unacceptable septic system; source of well water—unknown; no known source of income; head of household—single unwed female. Elizabeth Harnish, a thirteen-year-old white female, may no longer dwell at this designation, and will be removed forthwith by County of Chatham Family and Children Services on November 18, 1969 by five o'clock (5:00 P.M.), Eastern Standard Time.

I have set my seal invested with the power granted by the State of Georgia herewith.

Judge William Frank

When the sheriff finished reading, no one spoke. Then he did. "You'll need to sign where the X is, Miz Osaha. If you can't write, just make your mark." Josie picked up his pen and in well-formed letters signed, "Josephine Aija Oasaha." After the sheriff left, Josie put her arms around Tessie and Annie and they cried together, making the softsounds of rain and wind, called forth from their souls.

Josie spoke first. "I ain't gonna let them take you for very long, and I ain't gonna let them take you very far. You hear me, Tessie?" Tessie didn't hear her, instead she heard the sheriff's voice saying as he read "this residence is not acceptable for foster care," and she wanted to scream, "Why—too much love here, Sheriff?" She didn't register his departure any more than she registered Josie's words. And Josie knew Tessie was in trouble because her deep blue eyes shifted around the room—unable to light on anything—just like Josie had seen Laura Jean's do the day they came to take her away.

"Tessie...

"Tessie!"

Tessie heard Annie's voice—off in a distance. So she began to look for her and found herself as her eyes began to work again, found herself still at Josie's.

"Mama and I are right here. And we're going to figure something out, aren't we Mama?"

"Yes, baby, we are. I don't give one good goddamn about the judge and the court. But we got to be careful," and Josie stopped herself there. The Chatham County Sheriff had narrowed his eyes at Josie. He had taken out his notepad and pencil, and he looked like he was going to write down anything else she said. "We'll talk soon, Tessie. I promise." White, drunk and white, stupid and white would win over black and female, black and love, black Annie believed in her mother's strength and the power of her love for Elizabeth Harnish. Surely Family and Children Services couldn't be so blind to think that Tessie had to be with a white family who didn't know her over a black family that loved her.

The next day Family and Children's Services sent a woman from the orphanage with the same police officer. No one pretended anything, which meant no one spoke. Tessie hugged Annie and Josie goodbye and then carried her old blue suitcase filled with the objects of her life down the three stairs. The officer loaded the suitcase in the trunk, loaded Tessie in the backseat behind the cage, and drove away. Tessie felt like Ray looked when they arrested him.

In the backseat of the sheriff's car, Elizabeth Harnish looked about four, felt about ninety, her spirit aged zero. She was trapped and ready to run. Her heart kept beating the questions, "Isn't being thirteen supposed to be about being protected and free?" Family and Children Services placed Tessie in a foster home with a white family on the other side of Route 17 where she had to go to a different junior high school. The first thing she did after she was shown to her room and the people left her was to unpack her bag.

Tessie took the three cobalt blue jars that Laura Jean had bought for her for Christmas when she was 9. Laura Jean had wrapped each of them separately and put them in a box. She selected the most magical paper Newberry's had—white tissue with tiny red, green, and cobalt blue stars. She tied one with a red ribbon, one with a green ribbon, and one with dark blue ribbon, and then she placed them on under the Christmas tree. Tessie shook the boxes, but the only sound she heard was a thump. On Christmas morning, Tessie untied each bow, unfastened the tape, and folded the paper. She kept her face fixed with a smile, but the jars didn't make any sense to Tessie. After breakfast, Tessie asked her mother to help her iron out the wrinkles in the ribbons and the creases in the paper so it could be used again.

"Don't you like the jars, Tessie?" Laura Jean asked.

"I do, Mama. I just don't know what I am to use them for."

"To put pieces of the things you love in them, honey. That's what they are for. You know, like the feathers and bones, trinkets and broken glass you find."

"Maybe, Mama. I just don't like putting beautiful things away. The lids on the jars seal everything in too much, don't they, Mama? I love them, though. I love the blue glass. What color do you call that blue?"

"Cobalt, Tessie. Aren't they lovely, darlin'? They made me think of the river, the rain, the sky, and your eyes. And they are all for you. You can put anything your fluttering heart desires in them, fill them with magic potions or gather salamander eggs from the still water. Whatever you want. If they were mine, I'd leave them empty and hope they'd be filled by fairies while I slept. I'd leave them empty and try to fill them with my slippery dreams."

Tessie remembered hugging on her mother's neck that Christmas morning. She circled her arms around her and kept them there. She watched the pulse and smelled stale Evening in Paris perfume and old cigarettes. Laura Jean sang, "Hush little darling, don't say a word, Mama's gonna buy you a mockingbird." Tessie remembered asking her to sing Greensleeves or Silent Night instead, since it was Christmas, but her mother had kept on singing the other song.

Tessie's sadness was cobalt blue as she set each blue jar on her dresser. Her eyes, almost the color of the glass, considered the puzzle of three empty jars from her mother, three cobalt blue jars bought empty, wrapped empty, and now sitting empty on her dresser in a foster home.

THE WITCH DOCTOR
~ Olga Abella

One day Aunt Neida
ripped the clothes
from her body and ran
through the streets of Havana.
Her brothers and sisters
chased her between
the outhouses and pigpens.
When they caught her
they wrapped her in a blanket
to cover the shame.
They had to tie her to the bed
because she dug her nails
into her arms and legs
and kept trying to run away.
Days passed. She would not eat.
After a week three of them
dragged her to the witch doctor,
to the hut with its dangling beads,
black feathers and chicken claws.
My mother crossed herself
before she pushed
her crazy sister inside the door.
It took only ten minutes.
They were not allowed to see,
but Neida was fine after that,
except she never spoke again
and always hung around the children.

THE ROUNDING OF DOGS: COMING TO HERSELF
~ Olga Abella

Dogs used to be squares for her,
tables with four legs.
She drew dogs as parallelograms
with heads that had corners.
On mornings going to work she saw
her neighbor Sam walking
a brown rectangle dog around the block.
But those were days she didn't think
about insides,
living only on the surface of her skin
barely eating
breathing only because it happened.

That was before she met a dog, learned its name,
discovered he liked chocolate-covered peanuts,
to put his head on her lap and sleep on her bed.
She started seeing dogs had round parts
like paws and eyes, that they could
bend as they ran in circles
or curled next to her while she drank coffee.
She began understanding the ways of dogs,

and realized she was hungry, that she liked
the taste of kiwi and Oreos after dinner.
She moved inside her skin and saw how long
her arms were, how her hands were strong
enough to nail shingles on roofs, how her feet
did little jigs when she walked Ramsey
around the block and met Sam walking Charlie,
who liked peanut-butter cookies.

At night she dreamed of dogs
carrying her on their backs through forests
and deserts, while she gripped their fur
in her fists
and shielded the wind with their ears.

THE DREAM
~ Olga Abella

sometimes when the night air
        comes in with
                mucho cuidado *as if*

it were trying not to make itself known
i think it is you traveling from the dead
        on a blanket woven
like that orange cloud i saw once just
above the ocean where i used to imagine
you as a sailor when you were my father

     before you died i turned you into
     a stranger because *era mejor asi*
much better than trying to shape love into
something i could hold in my hand
that could burn like the orange in
that cloud above the ocean spreading
hot and thin below the top layer of my skin
so that i would never be able
to be me without you, to let go
of the heat waves of anger, the body waves
of hard touch

always the night air becomes too much to breathe
       as i try to make you go away

EVERYTHING COMES IN LIGHT TONIGHT
~ Maureen Shay

Like rain falling through trees,
through shadow, shadow and light

upon light: there are fireflies.
Mating is involved, and feeding.

I've seen a spider wrestle one
for an hour, the beetle not fazed

by the brightness of its own dying—
and dying. Old tales of changelings

say that when we do not sleep
breath becomes fireflies, while

Navaho say they channel
sun into night. This night

I feel the rain beneath my skin.
My friend has not been well

for some time. We take it slow,
sit among ferns on the porch

and talk in the dusk. His light
is more steady there, and when

the candle flies rise, we move
out and stand in a scattered

cloud of stars, two forms silent
and still on the soft wet lawn.

The trees drip but the sparks remain.
We take breath upon breath

under the oak canopy
and everything comes in light,

even the rain. We listen
to them glow. They say the same

thing dark as when they are bright.

CONTRIBUTORS' BIOGRAPHIES

Olga Abella teaches creative writing and literature at Eastern Illinois University. She received her BA from Southampton College at Long Island University, her MA and PhD from SUNY at Stony Brook. Her poems have appeared in *black dirt, CALYX, Urban Spaghetti, Natural Bridge, The MacGuffin, poetrybay.com, poetpourri, Long Island Quarterly, Kalliope* and others. She has published two chapbooks, *Grasping to What Is* (A Short Book Press, 1993) and *What It Takes* (Birnham Wood Graphics, 2000), and a recent book of poems *Watching the Wind* (Writers Ink Press 2008). She is editor of the literary journal *Bluestem.*

David Appelbaum is a hiker and biker, former editor of *Parabola Magazine* and publisher of Codhill Press whose work has appeared in such places as *APR, Commonweal, Verse Daily,* and *Rhino.*

Walter Bargen has published eleven books of poetry and two chapbooks. The latest are: *The Feast* (BkMk Press-UMKC, 2004), a series of prose poems, winner of the 2005 William Rockhill Nelson Award); *Remedies for Vertigo* (WordTech Communications, 2006); and *West of West* from (Timberline Press, 2007). *Theban Traffic* is scheduled for publication in 2008. His poems have recently appeared in the *Beloit Poetry Journal, New Letters, Poetry East,* and the *Seattle Review.* He was just appointed to be the first poet laureate of Missouri. www. WalterBargen.com

Jeanne Blum holds a Bachelor of Arts degree in French from DePauw University (cum laude, 1983). She enjoys wide-ranging interests, among them languages and literatures, art, music, and natural science. Over the years she has published four books, including *Bill Gates* (Lerner, 2007) and *MIAs* (ABC-CLIO, 1998), as well as hundreds of articles for magazines and reference books. Recently her poems have appeared in the anthology *Poem, Revised* and such journals as *The Tarwolf Review, Drash, Pennsylvania English* and *The Binnacle.* She invites correspondence via jeannemlesinski@gmail.com.

Reine Dugas Bouton teaches English at Southeastern Louisiana University. Scholarly interests include Eudora Welty, Louisiana literature, and the travel writing of Italy. Last year, she edited a collection of essays on Welty's *Delta Wedding*. Each summer, she takes students to study the literature and culture of Italy with Southeastern's study abroad program. Recent nonfiction has appeared in *Italy from a Backpack* and *Literary Mama Magazine*.

Ronda Broatch is the author of *Some Other Eden*, (Finishing Line Press, 2005). Nominated for the Pushcart Prize and Best of the Web, Ronda is the recipient of the 2005 Kay Snow Poetry Award, 2006 WPA William Stafford Award, and 2007 Artist Trust GAP Grant. Her work appeared recently on *Verse Daily*.

Derrick Weston Brown holds an MFA in Creative Writing from American University. He has studied poetry under Dr. Tony Medina at Howard University, Cornelius Eady and Henry Taylor at American University, and Sharon Olds at The Squaw Valley Summer Writers Retreat. He is a former Lannan Fellow and a Cave Canem fellow. His work has appeared in such literary journals as *Warpland, DrumVoices, The Columbia Review* and the online journals *Capital Beltway* and Howard University's *Amistad*. His work has also appeared in *The Washington Post* and *New Orleans Times-Picayune* newpapers and such anthologies as *When Words Become Flesh* (Mwaza Publications), *Taboo Haiku* (Avisson Press), and *Gathering Ground: A Reader Celebrating Cave Canem's First Decade* (University Of Michigan Press). In 2006 he released his first chapbook of poetry entitled *The Unscene* and has recently completed a full-length manuscript entitled *Gist*. He is a native of Charlotte North Carolina, and currently resides in Mount Rainier Maryland. He teaches two poetry classes at The Duke Ellington School Of Performing Arts in Washington D.C. He is the Poet-In-Residence at Busboys and Poets bookstore and restaurant, which is operated by the non-profit Teaching For Change.

Randall Brown teaches at Saint Joseph's University. He holds an MFA from Vermont College and a BA from Tufts. Recent work has appeared or is forthcoming in *Hunger Mountain, Connecticut Review, The Saint Ann's Review, The Evansville Review, The Laurel Review, Dalhousie Review*, and others. He's recently finished a collection of (very) short fiction, *Mad To Live*. Also, as an editor with *SmokeLong Quarterly,* he's had the pleasure of publishing short shorts by Dan Chaon, Steve Almond, Stuart Dybek, Sherrie Flick, Robert Shapard, Melanie Rae Thon, and many other exceptional writers. He's also had the privilege of working closely with some amazing teachers, including Douglas Glover, Abby Frucht, Nance Van Winckel, Tern-Brown Davidson, Ellen Lesser, Kathi Appelt, and Pamela Painter.

Adam Burnett lives and writes (whichever comes first) in Toronto, Ontario. He has had stories published in *Down in the Dirt, Rhapsoidia, Peeks and Valleys,* and *Midnight Times*. He is currently working on an Epic Poem entitled "Ode to a Pint of Guinness," which he swears he would have finished long ago if only he didn't keep finishing the pints first. He promises he'll never write a book in which any character belches for comedic effect.

Edward Butscher was born and raised in Flushing, Queens, taught for many years, wrote the first bios of Sylvia Plath (1976, reissued with new afterword by Schaffner Press in 2003), and Conrad Aiken, (winner of the PSA's Melville Cane Award in 1988), plus short critical books on Adelaide Crapsey (1979) and Peter Wild (1992). Poetry collections include *Amagansett Cycle* (1980) and *Child in the House* (1994). Also contributed to a number of reference works, among them, *MaGill's Survey of Contemporary Poetry* and the *Oxford Companion to Twentieth-Century Poetry in English*. Good obit fodder.

Michael Cadnum is an award-winning poet, a professional photographer, an amateur archaeologist, and he is learning new respect for spiders. He lives in Albany, California, with his wife Sherina.

Alan Catlin recently retired from his unchosen profession as a barman to devote more time to his written work. His most recent book of poetry is *Self-Portrait as the Artist Afraid of His Self-Portrait* from March Street Press.

Daniel Coshnear (dan@coshnear.org) lives in Guerneville, California with his wife and two children. He woks at a group home for men and women with mental illnesses and substance issues and he is author of a collection of stories, J*obs & Other Preoccupations* (Helicon Nine, 2000, Willa Cather Award winner).

Andrea Cumbo is a writer and writing teacher living in North East (yes, the town is called North East), Maryland. Her work has appeared or is forthcoming in *Science and Spirit, Santa Monica Review, South Loop Review,* and other publications. Currently, she balancing writing with the world of two new kittens and basement remodeling.

Phebe Davidson is a recovering academic, the author of twenty-some published collections of poems, a contributing editor at *Tar River Poetry* and a staff writer for *The Asheville Poetry Review.* Her newest book is *Waking to Light* (Main Street Rag Publishing Co., 2012)

Devin Wayne Davis, once called "ink (or inc.)" in an seaside vision, has written well over 2,000 poems; he likes concise verse. his work is printed in *the sacramento anthology: 100 poems; sanskrit; dwan; poetry depth quarterly; dandelion; coe review; rattlesnake; taproot;* and 38 chapbooks. selections can be found on-line, at these fine sites: *howling dog press; del sol review; wordslingers; perihelion; pierian springs; locust magazine; ginosko; kota press; octavo; lifix; jones av.; pig iron malt; great works; la petite zine; stirring; offcourse; rio arts; wandering dog; poems niederngasse; whimperbang; kookamonga square; wheelhouse; chiron review; eratio; split shot; poetry magazine; poetry monthly; fullosia; new verse news; penhimalaya; wordslaw; aurora review, muscadine lines; toe tree journal; pcm; down in the dirt; soma; tmp; haiku scotland; medusa's kitchen; spam;* and *zambomba.* thank you all. Davis has read as a feature poet at major book retailers; he has addressed citizens and lawmakers on the northern steps of the california state capitol, and has read for annual poetry events at the crocker art museum. davis reviewed movies for a best-selling paperback guide; he has written for sacramento, ca. arts & entertainment weeklies, and worked for ups and the state. Davis served in the u.s. army. he visited spain, germany, switzerland, france, and was last assigned to ft. bragg, n.c. as a photojournalist. Davis earned a bachelors degree in journalism and history. Davis has hiked mt. whitney three times. davis has three daughters, and has had testicular cancer. he's a leo. townee_towne@hotmail.com.

Sarah Dawson grew up in the sunny city of Durban on the east coast of South Africa. She was once a lifestyle journalist, is now a freelance writer, poet and student, and is trying to be a filmmaker. She is currently studying towards a masters degree in Film Studies in her home town.

jacob erin-cilberto, originally from Bronx, NY, now resides in Carbondale, Illinois. erin-cilberto has been writing and publishing poetry since 1970. He currently teaches at John A. Logan and Shawnee Community colleges in Southern Illinois.

His work has appeared in numerous small magazines and journals including: *Café Review, Skyline Magazine, Hudson View, Wind Journal, Pegasus, Parnassus* and others. erin-cilberto also writes reviews of poetry books for *Chiron Review, Skyline Review, Birchbrook Press* and others. He has reviewed books by B.Z Niditch, Michael Miller, Barry Wallenstein, Marcus Rome, musician Tom Maclear and others. *Used Lanterns* is erin-cilberto's 12th book of poetry and is now available through Water Forest Press, Stormville, NY. erin-cilberto has been nominated for a Pushcart Prize in Poetry in 2006-2007-2008 and again in 2010. He teaches poetry workshops for Heartland Writers Guild, Southern Illinois Writers Guild and Union County Writers Guild.

Rina Ferrarelli's work, original poetry and translation, has been collected in six books, the most recent, *The Bread We Ate* (Guernica), a collection of poems, and *Winter Fragments* (Chelsea), a translation of the lyrics of Bartolo Cattafi, a Sicilian poet. Her poems have been published in journals such as *Barrow Street, The Chariton Review, Chelsea, College English, 5 A.M., Laurel Review, The Pittsburgh Post-Gazette, Poet Lore, Runes, Tar River Poetry, VIA,* and in dozens of anthologies and textbooks.

Fred Ferraris books: *The Durango Chronicles, Book One* (Blue Marmot Press, 2004), *Older Than Rain* (Selva Editions, 1997), *Marpa Point* (Blackberry Books, 1976) *Anthologies: Prayers for a Thousand Years* (Harper, 1999).
Journals: Audience, *Cafe Irreal, Caveat Lector, Cold Mountain Review, Diner, Heaven Bone, Mad Blood, Marginalia, Orbis, Soundings East, Spout, Switched-On Gutenberg, thieves jargon, Wavelength, Worcester Review, Yalobusha Review.*

Karen K. Ford was born & raised in the City of Orange, in Southern California. She began her writing career in high-school, as editor-in-chief of the Villa Park *Oracle,* and later put herself through Cal State Fullerton by freelancing ad copy. She moved to Ashland, Oregon in 1989 and worked as marketing director for a small winery (some grape stomping was involved) and, later, for a manufacturer of high-end audio equipment, where she mostly kept her shoes on. After 13 years in Southern Oregon she returned to Los Angeles to pursue fiction writing full-time. She lives in Mandeville Canyon with her husband, writer S.L. Stebel, and their rescue mutt, Dude. She is a contributing editor for *American Salon* magazine, and her short stories have appeared in *Goliards* and *Man's Story 2.* She is the winner of *Narrative Magazine's* Winter 2013 fiction prize and two-time winner of the excellence in writing award from the Santa Barbara Writers Conference. Her debut novel, *Salvage,* is currently being offered for publication.

Carol Graser lives in the Adirondacks of upstate New York. She has read her poetry at many community events including fund-raisers, anti-war rallies and as a featured reader at poetry events around NY state. She hosts a monthly poetry reading series at Saratoga's historic

Caffe Lena that happens on the first Wednesday of every month. Her poetry has appeared in regional journals such as *Screed, Salvage* and *Metroland* as well as in numerous national publications like *Lullwater Review, Berkeley Poetry Review, The Worcester Review, The MacGuffin* and *Eureka Literary Magazine.*

Jonathan Greenhause is the winner of *Prism Review*'s 2012-2013 Poetry Prize and finalist for this year's Gearhart Poetry Contest from *The Southeast Review.* He has received two Pushcart nominations and is the author of a chapbook, *Sebastian's Relativity* (Anobium Books, 2011). His poetry has recently appeared or is forthcoming in *Hawai'i Pacific Review, The Midwest Quarterly, The Moth* (IRE), *Popshot* (UK), *Regime* (AUS), *Sugar House Review,* and elsewhere. Currently, he and his wife are being raised by their newborn son, Benjamin Seneca.

RG Gregory—born Southampton UK 1928. Grammar School evacuee (39-45); Army conscript 46-49—Sgt Education Corps; King's College, London—English degree (52); teacher (English and Drama) 19 years—Hampshire, Uganda, Shropshire (53-72), running innovative educational practices; Founder member Word And Action (Dorset)—community and touring theatre and language-arts company (72-03)—performances in over 20 countries, including Israel, Thailand, Japan, Australia and the US (Birmingham and San Francisco; now live in Shropshire in late third relationship. Six children (one dead). Prolific poet—publications *Glimpses of Dorset, Christmas Delinquent, Gentlemen lift the sea* (and other selections. collections, sequences not published; countless poems in small magazines; over 800 poem-graphics; over 20 plays (for performance in-the-round); novel and short stories; *The World of Instant Theatre, Through the Circle, The Group Dream* (130 stories from Instant Theatre performances, with commentaries), plus pamphlets on individual IT stories from courses run in several countries; now working with small local poetry-writing group (all women, aged 60+) contributing to magazine *Tuesday Treasury* and giving local readings and performances of its work. Also engaged in writing book on the driving intentions of all he has done in the literary and dramatic fields for the past 70 years.

Lisa Harris writes poetry, fiction, and essays. She has a Master of Fine Arts from Milton Avery Graduate School and holds other degrees in educational leadership, literature and literacy. Born of German and English descent in the Allegheny Moutntains of Pennsylvania, she has lived in Savannah, Georgia and Trumansburg, New York. Her fictions have been published by Bright Hill Press, Westview/Harpercollins, *ginosko, The Distillery, MacGuffin, RiversEdge, Nimrod International, Stillwater, The American Aesthetic, Argestes, The Habersham Review, Phoebe, Zone 3, The Coe Review, cantaraville,* and *Anemone Sidecar.* Her poetry has been published in *The Second Word Thursday Anthology, Puerto del Sol, The Cathartic, Karamu, Stillwater, Fennel Stalk,* and exhibited in collaborative word and image installations with Susan Weisend, Nancy Valle and Carol Spence.

Christopher Hart contends that writing is the most pleasurable activity that a person can pursue on a lazy afternoon. His short stories have been published in a number of literary journals, including *The Speculative Edge* and *Inwood, Indiana.*

Lisa Haviland journals: *Another America, Dufus, Other, Pedestal Magazine, Poetry Superhighway, Wicked Alice.* hazeablaze.blogspot.com

Thomas Hedlund: Several years following his graduation from Michigan State University in East Lansing, Michigan with a BA in Psychology. He has earned honors for his short story "Power Windows" in *The Writer's Journal,* a national publication, has published several articles, poems, and other fiction in publications and collections such as *More Sugar, Painted in the Forest,* and *Immortal Verses.* His story "Ripples" appeared in the spring 2006 issue of *The Storyteller.* He was a contributing member of Morningside Writers Group based in New York City, a professional network of writers and editors, for six years. Enrolled in an MFA in Creative Writing program at National University and earning honors in the process with an emphasis on Screenwriting. www.GThomasHedlund.com.

Stephen Kessler is the author, most recently, of *Burning Daylight* (poems, Littoral Press); his translation (with Daniela Hurezanu) of *Eyeseas*, poems by Raymond Queneau, is due this summer from Black Widow Press, and his book of essays *Moving Targets: On Poets, Poetry & Translation* will be issued in the fall by El León Literary Arts. He is a contributing editor of *Poetry Flash* and the editor of *The Redwood Coast Review.*

Pete Lee's fiction has appeared in *In Tenebris Lux, At Play, An Anthology of Maine Drama, The Licking River Review, Maine Lawyers Review, The Connecticut Review* and will appear shortly in *Nerve Cowboy.* In the daylight hours, he is a lawyer in private practice. Currently, he is at work on a longer piece of (as yet) undetermined length entitled *Call Him Lenny.* Pete lives in Yarmouth, Maine with his wife, Lynne, and their two sons, Spence and Travis.

Fraida Liba Levine earned her BA in English from UCLA, with a concentration in creative writing. She served as assistant poetry editor on the staff of *Westwind*, UCLA's Literary Journal. Fraida Liba has contributed poetry to *Transformation, Westwind, Vulcan, The Kerf, Heartlodge, Pepperdine University's Expressionists, Fusion Literary Magazine,* and Hunter College's *Olivetree Review.* She lives in Los Angeles with her husband and her three children.

Joneve McCormick's poetry, articles and short stories have been published in a wide variety of hard copy and online literary and art periodicals and in several poetry anthologies. *Small Bird Bones*, a solo collection of poems, was published by The New Press (NYC) in 1993. Recently she edited the international anthology of poetry, *World's Strand* (academici, UK), for publication. She hosts online journals, *Soul to Soul* and *The Peregrine Muse.*

Jay Michaelson is the founding editor of *Zeek: A Jewish Journal of Thought and Culture,* a columnist for the *Forward,* and the author of *God in Your Body: Kabbalah, Mindfulness, and Embodied Spiritual*

Practice. His work has appeared in *Slate, The Jerusalem Post, Blithe House Quarterly, Blueline, White Crane, and Beliefnet, and in anthologies including Mentsh: On Being Jewish and Queer* and Righteous *Indignation: A Jewish Call for Justice.* He lives in upstate New York.

Susan Niz has published with *Cezanne's Carrot, The Summerset Review, flashquake,* and *Opium Magazine.* Her short fiction is set in Guatemala and inspired by her husband's childhood. She has written a novel set in her native Minneapolis. It is yet unpublished. She is finding new and miraculous sources of inspiration these days. Links to her published writing can be found at susannizfiction.blogspot.com

Jane Ormerod was born on the south coast of England and moved from London to New York City in 2004. Her work appears in numerous US and UK publications including *21 Stars Review, Arsenic Lobster, eratio postmodern poetry, failbetter,* and *Word Riot.* A spoken word CD, *Nashville Invades Manhattan,* was released in 2007 and an anthology, *A Cautionary Tale: Peer into the Lives of Seven New York Performing Poets* (Uphook Press), will be published in early 2008. A regular on the New York live poetry circuit, in January 2007 Jane toured the west coast—Vancouver, Canada, down to San Francisco—as part of the Perpetual Motion Roadshow. Recently she returned to California for more readings and an interview on KFJC Radio. Her website is www.JaneOrmerod.com.

Born in post-revolutionary Cuba in the sixties, **Alix Reeves**' family fled to South Pasadena, California. She attended California State University at Los Angeles where she received her Master of Science Degree in Psychology. Widowed at a young age, she began to write prolifically, in an attempt to manage grief. She was driven to explore the little-known experience of the children of pedophiles, which inspired her first screenplay, *Why Things Burn,* a finalist at The Sundance Institute of Film, winner of the Key West IndieFest, finalist at both the London Independent Film Festival and the Beverly Hills Film Festival. Her most recent screenplay, a children's comedy written for animation, won the Kid's First Screenplay Competition and is currently a finalist at the Screenwriting Expo. She signed with Santa Fe Films in 2008. Happily engaged, she lives both in Milwaukee, WI, and Pasadena, CA, with her fiancé Todd and their daughter Lydia.

Tree Riesener has published poetry and short fiction in numerous literary magazines, including *Flashquake, Flash Fiction Online, Litsnack, The Evergreen Review, Loch Raven Review, Pindeldyboz, Identity Theory, The Belletrist Review,* and *The Source.* Her achievements include three first prizes for the Short-Short Story and the Literary Short Story at the Philadelphia Writers Conference, Finalist for Black Lawrence Press's Hudson Prize, Finalist in *PANK* magazine's Fiction Chapbook Contest, Best of *Wigleaf* 2009 (Honorable Mention), Semi-Finalist in the Pablo Neruda Competition, three short stories staged in the Writing Aloud productions of InterAct Theatre, Philadelphia, a Hawthornden International Writing Fellowship, two Pushcart nominations, and the William Van Wert Fiction Award. She is the author of three poetry collections, *Inscapes, Angel Poison* and *Liminalog.* Her website is www.TreeRiesener.com and she blogs at treeriesener.blogspot.com.

Suzanne Roberts is the author of three books of poetry, *Shameless* (2007), *Nothing to You* (2008), and *Plotting Temporality* (forthcoming from Red Hen Press). She writes and teaches in South Lake Tahoe, California. For more information, please visit her website at www.SuzanneRoberts.org.

P. Alanna Roethle is a writer, editor, and photographer based in Austin, TX and Tucson, AZ. She has had poems and short stories published in several online magazines and print publications/anthologies and is currently writing a memoir about growing up on the road. www.RoadsOnHerFace.com.

Natalie Safir has been publishing poems in national literary journals since the 1980s and anthologized in college texts: Her books published are *Moving into Seasons,* 1981, *To Face the Inscription,* 1987, *Made*

Visible in 1998, and *A Clear Burning* in 2004.. She teaches Writing as Healing at the Hudson Valley Writers Center and is a certified coach and gestalt therapist.

Craig Saunders lives in Norfolk, England, with his wife and three children, who he pretends to listen to while making up stories in his head. He holds a degree in Japanese, and lived in Japan for five years where he held a number of jobs; editor, translator, and carpenter among them. He knows enough jujitsu, karate, aikido and kendo to be a danger only to himself.

He has published more than two dozen short stories, and is the author of many novels including *Rain* (Crowded Quarantine Publications), *The Love of the Dead* (Evil Jester Press) and *A Stranger's Grave* (Grand Mal Press). He writes horror and fantasy for fun and humour when he's feeling serious, which isn't often. He blogs at craigrsaunders.blogspot.com.

Yvette A Schnoeker-Shorb   Anthologies: *The Blueline Anthology* (Syracuse University Press, 2004), *90 Poets of the Nineties: An Anthology of American and Canadian Poets* (Seminole Press, 1998) Journals: *Clackamas Literary Review, Entelechy, Eureka Literary MagaMagazine, Poem, Puerto del Sol, Slant: A Journal of Poetry, Terrain.org: A Journal of the Built & Natural Environments, Weber Studies, Wild Earth.zine, Green Hills Literary Lantern, Hawai'i Pacific Review, Karamu, Midwest Quarterly, Pedestal.*

EM Schorb's work has appeared in *The Southern Review, The Sewanee Review, Southwest Review, The Yale Review, The Chicago Review, Carolina Quarterly, The Virginia Quarterly Review, The Texas Review, The American Scholar, Stand* (England), *Agenda* (England), *Poetry Salzburg Review* (Austria), *The Sewanee Review, The Notre Dame Review, 5 AM, Rattle, Shenandoah, The New York Quarterly,* and many others. His collection, *Murderer's Day* (Purdue University Press), was awarded the Verna Emery Poetry Award. His most recent novel is *Fortune Island. Carbons: a Career in Letters,* and *Reflections in a Doubtful I,* a collection of verse, are just out.

Nina Sharma's work has been featured in *Certain Circuits Magazine, The Feminist Wire, Ginosko Literary Journal,* and *Reverie: Midwest African American Literature.* She recently was awarded a fellowship from the Vermont Studio Center and nominated for a Pushcart Prize for her nonfiction. With Quincy Scott Jones, she co-created the Nor'easter Exchange: a multicultural, multi-city reading series. She is currently enrolled in Columbia University's MFA in writing program.

Maureen Shay lives and writes in Salisbury, North Carolina. She is currently an English teacher at Salisbury High School, where she has also taught Theatre Arts and where she encourages young people to investigate their interests in creative expression. Her poetry has appeared in *Tar River Poetry,* as well as in anthologies such as *Mountain Time* and *Wildacres Poetry.*

Larissa Shmailo has recently been published in and/ or heard on *About: Poetry, The Facebook Review, Babel, Big Bridge, Fulcrum, CLWN WR,* Naropa's *We (Creative Cannabilism), i-Outlaw, Nefarious Bovine Radio, Wordsalad,* and many other media. (please see www.myspace.com/thenonetworld for a complete listing). Her poetry CD, *The No-Net World,* has been heard on radio and Internet stations around the world. Larissa translated the Russian Futurist opera *Victory over the Sun* which was performed at theaters and museums internationally; a DVD of the original English-language production is part of the collection of the New York Museum of Modern Art. She is a director of *TWiN Poetry,* an informal collective of 7,000 audio poets, and a translator for the international poetry organization UniVerse. This year, she contributed translations to the anthology *New Russian Poetry* published by Dalkey Archive Press. She is pleased to join the masthead this year of the acclaimed annual *Fulcrum* as public coordinator.

Robert Joe Stout Books: *They Still Play Baseball the Old Way* (White Eagle Coffee Store Press, 1994), *The Blood of the Serpent* (Algora, 1994), *Swallowing Dust* (Red Hill Press, 1976), *Miss Sally* (Bobbs-Merrill,

1973). Journals: *Beloit Poetry Journal, Confluence, Georgetown Review, Interim, Mid-American Poetry Review, South Dakota Review, Whetstone* .

B R Strahan Books: *Crocodile Man* (The Smith, 1990) Anthologies: *Blood to Remember, American Poets on the Holocaust* (Texas Tech University Press, 2006), *Who Is Who, Poet's Collection* (Struga Poetry Evenings, 2003) Journals: *America, Christian Century, Confrontation, CrossCurrents, First Things, Hollins Critic, Margie, Onthebus, Rattapallax, Seattle Review, Soundings East, Southern California Anthology, Sun Dog.*

John Sweet, b. 1968, single father of 2. believer in writing as catharsis. eater of souls. plenty of tummy-ticklin' fun to be found at blog. myspace.bleedinghorsedenied.com

Jerry Vilhotti: I graduated from the only college that won the NIT and NCCA basketball tournaments in the same year but more importantly than that, Jonas Salk, who helped rid some of the world of polio with his vaccine was also given the opportunity to contribute to Mankind and graduated from the same NYC school that's called in some circles "The poor man's Harvard"; this and the fact that there was a place of higher learning that indeed gave every race, nationality and creed an opportunity to play in the game of sculpting a better world gives me greater joy. To use an analogy: I was a pretty good ballplayer in my day: I could hit singles, doubles and triples and sometimes home runs! I hit balls for fly outs or ground outs and sometimes I even struck out! That's how I feel like a writer-no more no less. I have been fortunate to have had stories published in the USA, Greece, India, Scotland, Ireland, England, Canada Singapore...many of which were literary magazines. I now live among the Litchfield Hills, in a simpler place in time, with the ghosts of Mark Twain in the east, Harriet Beecher Stowe on the west and John Brown to the north. I am with a beautiful wife who treats me well and waits for me to return from my imaginary meandering and we both helped—I swears to God!—in bringing three sort of nice kids into this world of whom we are very proud and I hope find loved ones as good as I found once a time ago.

Donna D Vitucci helps raise funds for local nonprofits, while her head and heart are engaged in the lives of the characters mounting a coup in her head. If her eyes appear vacant, you'll know she's in her alternate universe, following her "people" as they muck up their lives. Her stories can be found in dozens of print and online journals. Recent work appears, or is forthcoming, in *Salt River Review, Front Porch Journal, The Whitefish Review, Diner, Storyglossia, Cezanne's Carrot, Boston Literary Magazine, Insolent Rudder,* and *Another Chicago Magazine.*

Gunta Krasts Voutyras was born in Liepaja, Latvia. Am mult-lingual, a writer and a fiber artist. Spent the start of WW II in underground trenches in my parents' homestead. Due to politics of the time were sent with my family, minus my father, to Nazi Germany. Traveled across the Baltic sea in the hold of a Nazi hospital ship. With the horses. Criss-crossed Germany in cattle cars with the doors bolted from the outside. Periodically we were dumped off in Nazi detention camps, situated in the same way as Dachau, without the ovens. Treatment of all of us refugees was inhuman. Mass showers, our hair washed with gasoline, cold water for the so-called "shower", beatings, rotten potatoes cooked in water as our once a day meal. Once the war ended we found ourselves in the American Zone, in a Displaced Persons Camp in Esslingen am/ Neckar. From there traveled to USA under a law issued by Pres. Harry Truman. With a fine-tooth comb UNRRA (United Nations Relif and Rehabilitation Agency) scrutinized our health, education, intellect, political affiliations of the past, our goals. In 1949 arrived in New York without a word of English. And with thirty dollars between five of us given to us by the Church World Service. Went to public schools in New York City. After graduation from High School married. Have two grown children. I started writing in the DP Camps, at age eleven. At that time wrote poems, short biographical essays. My passion was and is reading. Am published on the Internet in *Helium.com, Poetry.com,* in Hugh Downs' last book, *My America,* have essays in various other venues. Am working on a novel.

Robert Wexelblatt is professor of humanities at Boston University's College of General Studies. He has published essays, stories, and poems in a wide variety of journals, two story collections, *Life in the Temperate Zone* and *The Decline of Our Neighborhood*, a book of essays, *Professors at Play*; his novel, *Zublinka Among Women*, won the Indie Book Awards First Prize for Fiction. His most recent book is a short novel, *Losses*.

Kelley Jean White studied at Dartmouth College and Harvard Medical School and worked as a pediatrician in inner-city Philadelphia for more than twenty-five years. Mother of three, she is an active Quaker, and has recently returned to her small New Hampshire village and begun work at a rural health center in the North Country. Her poems have been widely published over the past decade, in journals including *Exquisite Corpse, Nimrod, Poet Lore, Rattle* and the *Journal of the American Medical Association* and in several chapbooks and full-length collections. She is the recipient of a 2008 Pennsylvania Council on the Arts grant in poetry.

Dr. **Ernest Williamson III** has published poetry and visual art in over 400 national and international online and print journals. Some of Dr. Williamson's visual art and/or poetry has been published in journals representing over 40 colleges and universities around the world. Dr. Williamson is an adjunct professor, self-taught pianist, poet, singer, composer, social scientist, private tutor, and a self-taught painter. His poetry has been nominated three times for the *Best of the Net Anthology* (www.SundressPublications.com). The poems which were nominated for the *Best of the Net Anthology* were as follows: "The Jazz of Old Wine", "The Symbol of Abiotic Needs", & "The Misfortune of Shallow Sight". He holds the B.A. and the M.A. in English/Creative Writing/Literature from the University of Memphis and the PhD in Higher Education Leadership from Seton Hall University. Dr. Williamson is also a chess master with a rating of 2203.